元詩明理接千載

古今抒情詩三百首
漢英對照

arallel Reading of 300 Ancient and Modern Chinese Lyrical Poems (Chinese-English)：Jin, Yuan, and Ming Dynasties

著者：林明理　Author: Dr. Lin Ming-Li
譯者：張智中　Translator: Prof. Zhang Zhizong

天空數位圖書出版

著者簡介
About the Author & Poet

　　學者詩人林明理博士〈1961-〉,臺灣雲林縣人,法學碩士、榮譽文學博士。她曾任教於大學,是位詩人評論家,擅長繪畫及攝影,著有詩集、散文、詩歌評論等文學專著34本書,包括在義大利合著的譯詩集 4 本。其詩作被翻譯成法語、西班牙語、義大利語、俄語及英文等多種,作品發表於報刊及學術期刊等已達兩千三百餘篇。中國學刊物包括《南京師範大學文學院學報》等多篇。

　　Dr. Lin Mingli (1961-), poet and scholar, born in Yunlin County, Taiwan, Master of Law, honorary Ph. D. in literature. She once taught at a university and is a poetry critic, and she is good at painting and photography. She is the author of 33 literary books, including poetry collections, prose, and poetry reviews, as well as a collection of translated poems co-authored and published in Italy. Her poems have been translated into French, Spanish, Italian, Russian and English, etc., and over 2,300 poems and articles have been published in newspapers and academic journals.

*林明理專書 monograph、義大利出版的中英譯詩合著
Chinese-English Poetry Co-author published in Italy
Lin Ming-Li's monographs and co-authored Chinese-English Poetry collections published in Italy

1. 《秋收的黃昏》Dusk of Autumn Harvest
2. 《夜櫻－林明理詩畫集》Night Cherry - Lin Ming-Li's Poetry Collection
3. 《新詩的意象與內涵－當代詩家作品賞析》The Image and Connotation of New poetry — Appreciation of Contemporary Poets
4. 《藝術與自然的融合－當代詩文評論集》The Fusion of Art and Nature — Contemporary Poetry Review
5. 《山楂樹》Hawthorn Tree
6. 《回憶的沙漏》The Hourglass of Memory
7. 《湧動著一泓清泉－現代詩文評論》A Fresh Spring Flowing — Modern Poetry Review
8. 《清雨塘》Qing Yu Tang
9. 《用詩藝開拓美－林明理讀詩》Using Poetry Art to Develop Beauty — Lin Ming-Li's Poetry Reading
10. 《海頌－林明理詩文集》Hymn to the Sea — Collection of Lin Ming-Li's Poems
11. 《林明理報刊評論 1990-2000》Lin Ming-Li's Newspaper Review 1990-2000
12. 《行走中的歌者－林明理談詩》Walking Singer — Lin Ming-Li's Poems
13. 《山居歲月》Living in the Mountain
14. 《夏之吟》Summer Yin
15. 《默喚》Inspiration
16. 《林明理散文集》Lin Ming-Li's Essays
17. 《名家現代詩賞析》Famous Modern Poetry Appreciation
18. 《我的歌》My Song
19. 《諦聽》Listening
20. 《現代詩賞析》Modern Poetry Appreciation

21. 《原野之聲》 The Sound of the Field
22. 《思念在彼方　散文暨新詩》Missing in the Other Side of the Prose and New Poetry
23. 《甜蜜的記憶(散文暨新詩)》Sweet Memory (Prose and new poetry)
24. 《詩河(詩評、散文暨新詩)》，文史哲出版社。Poetry River (Poetry Criticism, prose and new poetry), History & Philosophy Publishing House.
25. 《庫爾特‧F‧斯瓦泰克，林明理，喬凡尼‧坎皮西詩選》（中英對照）Selected Poems by Kurt F. Swatek, Lin Ming-Li and Giovanni Campisi (Chinese-English)
26. 《紀念達夫尼斯和克洛伊》（中英對照）詩選，義大利：Edizioni Universum（埃迪采恩尼大學），宇宙出版社。Selected Poems in Memory of Davonis and Chloe (Chinese-English), Italy: Edizioni Universum (University of Ediceni), Cosmos Press.
27. 《詩林明理古今抒情詩 160 首》Parallel Reading of 160 Ancient and Modern Chinese Lyrical Poems (Chinese-English)
28. 《愛的讚歌》(詩評、散文暨新詩) Hymn of Love (Poetry commentary, prose and New poems)
29. 《埃內斯托‧卡漢，薩拉‧錢皮，林明理和平詩選》（義英對照）Selected Poems of Ernesto Kahan, Sara Ciampi, Lin Mingli and Heping (Yi-Ying contrast)
30. 《祈禱與工作》（中英義詩集 Prayer and Work
31. 《名家抒情詩評賞》（漢英對照）Appreciation of Lyrical Poems by Famous Poets (Chinese-English)
32. 《山的沉默》Silence of the Mountains
33. 《宋詩明理接千載——古今抒情詩三百首》（漢英對照）Parallel Reading of 300 Ancient and Modern Chinese Lyrical Poems (Chinese-English).
34. 《元詩明理接千載——古今抒情詩三百首》（漢英對照）Parallel Reading of 300 Ancient and Modern Chinese Lyrical Poems (Chinese-English): Jin, Yuan, and Ming Dynasties.

譯者簡介
About the Author & Translator

　　張智中，天津市南開大學外國語學院教授、博士研究生導師、翻譯系主任，中國翻譯協會理事，中國英漢語比較研究會典籍英譯專業委員會副會長，天津師範大學跨文化與世界文學研究院兼職教授，世界漢學‧文學中國研究會理事兼英文秘書長，天津市比較文學學會理事，第五屆天津市人民政府學位委員會評議組成員、專業學位教育指導委員會委員，國家社科基金專案通訊評審專家和結項鑒定專家，天津外國語大學中央文獻翻譯研究基地兼職研究員，《國際詩歌翻譯》季刊客座總編，《世界漢學》英文主編，《中國當代詩歌導讀》編委會成員，中國當代詩歌獎評委等。已出版編、譯、著120餘部，發表學術論文130餘篇，曾獲翻譯與科研多種獎項。漢詩英譯多走向國外，獲國際著名詩人和翻譯家的廣泛好評。
譯詩觀：但為傳神，不拘其形，散文筆法，詩意內容；將漢詩英譯提高到英詩的高度。

譯者簡介

Zhang Zhizhong is professor, doctoral supervisor and dean of the Translation Department of the School of Foreign Studies, Nankai University which is located in Tianjin; meanwhile, he is director of Translators' Association of China, vice chairman of the Committee for English Translation of Chinese Classics of the Association for Comparative Studies of English and Chinese, part-time professor of Cross-Culture & World Literature Academy of Tianjin Normal University, director and English secretary-general of World Sinology·Literary China Seminar, director of Tianjin Comparative Literature Society, member of Tianjin Municipal Government Academic Degree Committee, member of Tianjin Municipal Government Professional Degree Education Guiding Committee, expert for the approval and evaluation of projects funded by the National Social Science Foundation of China, part-time researcher at the Central Literature Translation Research Base of Tianjin Foreign Studies University, guest editor of *Rendition of International Poetry*, English editor-in-chief of *World Sinology*, member of the editing board of *Guided Reading Series in Contemporary Chinese Poetry*, and member of the Board for Contemporary Chinese Poetry Prizes. He has published more than 120 books and 130 academic papers, and he has won a host of prizes in translation and academic research. His English translation of Chinese poetry is widely acclaimed throughout the world, and is favorably reviewed by international poets and translators. His view on poetry translation: spirit over form, prose enjambment to rewrite Chinese poetry into sterling English poetry.

以詩代序[1]

古今詩詞明理續！
中外合璧智中翻。
文壇新章留佳話！
古今中外千載帆[2]。

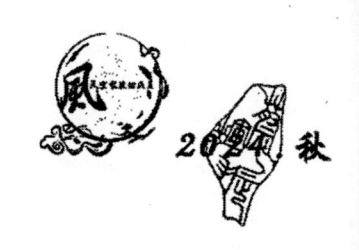

風 2024 秋

---
[1] 為作者林明理，譯者張智中：《元詩明理接千載》所題，並基於〝古今中外〞及作者、譯者名字所限，無從顧及平仄問題。
[2] 一帆風順，承載千年之意。

以詩代序

A Poem as Preface

Ancient Chinese poems are coupled by Lin Ming-Li;

a pair after another pair are translated by Zhang Zhizhong.

Creative writing & innovative translating for masterpieces;

modernization & globalization of lyrical Chinese poems.

By Tsai Huei-Ching
The autumn of 2024

元詩明理耀千載
古今詩情詩三百首 漢英對照

著者暨編譯者導言
Introduction by the Compiler-Translator

學者詩人林明理從她自己所感覺到的與對古詩閱讀的經驗回憶裡進行篩選、組合，欲使其創作的詩歌加在編譯的元詩絕句之後，以期望讀者更貼近地感覺和瞭解詩美的世界。而我認為，若能讓古詩和新詩研究同步相輔相成，讓翻譯詩歌的涵義變得更生動活潑，以趨使學生對欣賞詩歌與研讀上產生了更大的興趣，這是此書最重要的價值，也可以加深閱讀時的感性和體悟，這也是我的期許。

張智中教授
於 2024 年 11 月 1 日於南開大學外國語學院翻譯系

    Lin Ming-Li, as a scholar-poet of Taiwan, is a great lover of poetry, and she selects her own poems to be paired up with the quatrains by Chinese poets of Jin, Yuan, and Ming dynasties, which have similar themes or sentiments, in order for readers to appreciate more thoroughly the beauty of poetry. It is my belief that, if the reading and translation of both ancient Chinese poems and modern Chinese poems can be undertaken simultaneously, the understanding of poetry will be deepened, and poetry translation will be more flexible through enlivening — and the readers' interest in poetry, hopefully, will be greatly heightened.

Zhang Zhizhong
November 1, 2024
Translation Department of the School of Foreign Studies,
Nankai University

願我的愛像陽光一樣環繞著你，
賜予你輝煌的自由。
（印度詩人泰戈爾）

Let my love, like sunlight, surround you and yet give you illumined freedom.
— By Rabindranath Tagore, Indian Poet

目錄
Table of Contents

▶ 金朝 Jin Dynasty

1. 雞鳴山下橋（趙秉文）A Bridge Under the Cockcrow Mountain (Zhao Bingwen)
   山楂樹（林明理）Hawthorn Tree (Lin Ming-Li) ⋯⋯⋯⋯⋯ 28
2. 溪行（李庭）Strolling Along the Creek (Li Ting)
   淡水紅毛城之歌（林明理）Fortress San Domingo, Song of Danshui (Lin Ming-Li)⋯⋯⋯⋯⋯⋯⋯⋯⋯⋯⋯⋯ 30
3. 絕句（王庭筠）A Quatrain (Wang Tingjun)
   想妳，在墾丁（林明理）I Miss You, in Kending (Lin Ming-Li) ⋯⋯⋯⋯⋯⋯⋯⋯⋯⋯⋯⋯⋯⋯⋯⋯⋯ 32
4. 嗅梅圖（李仲略）The Picture of Smelling Plum Flowers (Li Zhonglüe)
   在我窗前起舞（林明理）Dancing in Front of My Window (Lin Ming-Li) ⋯⋯⋯⋯⋯⋯⋯⋯⋯⋯⋯⋯⋯⋯ 34
5. 不出（劉仲尹）To Stay Home (Liu Zhongyin)
   那年冬夜（林明理）That Winter Night (Lin Ming-Li) ⋯⋯ 36
6. 自理（劉仲尹）Self-help (Liu Zhongyin)
   我的夢想（林明理）My Dream (Lin Ming-Li) ⋯⋯⋯⋯⋯ 38
7. 寒夜（劉仲尹）The Cold Night (Liu Zhongyin)
   綠淵潭（林明理）Green Deep Pond (Lin Ming-Li) ⋯⋯⋯ 39
8. 初秋夜涼（劉仲尹）The Cold Night of Early Autumn (Liu Zhongyin)
   星河（林明理）The River of Stars (Lin Ming-Li) ⋯⋯⋯⋯ 41
9. 夏日（劉仲尹）The Summer Day (Liu Zhongyin)
   夏日慵懶的午後（林明理）A Languid Summer Afternoon (Lin Ming-Li) ⋯⋯⋯⋯⋯⋯⋯⋯⋯⋯⋯⋯⋯⋯⋯⋯⋯ 42

目錄

10. 一室（劉仲尹）A Solitary Room (Liu Zhongyin)
    林中小徑的黃昏（林明理）The Dusk of a Path in the Forest
    (Lin Ming-Li) ·· 44
11. 二月十一日見桃花（高士談）At the First Sight of Peach
    Flowers (Gao Shitan)
    布拉格猶太人墓園（林明理）The Jewish Cemetery in
    Prague (Lin Ming-Li) ·· 46
12. 楊花（高士談）Willow Filaments (Gao Shitan)
    流蘇花開（林明理）Tassel Flowering (Lin Ming-Li) ·········· 48
13. 雪（高士談）Snow (Gao Shitan)
    夜讀《帶著愛去斯基亞索斯島 TO SKIATHOS WITH
    LOVE》（林明理）Night reading *TO SKIATHOS WITH LOVE*
    (Lin Ming-Li) ·· 50
14. 睡起（高士談）Awake From a Sleep (Gao Shitan)
    加路蘭的晨歌（林明理）The Morning Song of Garulan
    (Lin Ming-Li) ·· 53
15. 道中（高士談）En Route (Gao Shitan)
    愛是一種光亮（林明理）Love Is a Kind of Light
    (Lin Ming-Li) ·· 55
16. 偶題（高士談）An Impromptu Piece (Gao Shitan)
    那年冬天（林明理）That Winter (Lin Ming-Li) ················ 57
17. 同兒輩賦未開海棠二首（其一）（元好問）Crabapple
    Flowers Before Blosssoming (No. 1) (Yuan Haowen)
    飛吧，我的蜂鳥（林明理）Keep Flying, My Hummingbird
    (Lin Ming-Li) ·· 59
18. 同兒輩賦未開海棠二首（其二）（元好問）Crabapple
    Flowers Before Blosssoming (No. 2) (Yuan Haowen)
    我的書房（林明理）My Study (Lin Ming-Li) ···················· 61
19. 論詩三十首（其四）（元好問）Poems on Poetry
    Composition (No. 4) (Yuan Haowen)
    愛無疆域（林明理）Love Is Boundless (Lin Ming-Li) ········ 64

13

20. 論詩三十首（其十二）（元好問）Poems on Poetry Composition (No. 12) (Yuan Haowen)
   傾聽紅松籽飄落（林明理）Listen to Red Pine Seeds Dropping Down (Lin Ming-Li) ……………… 66

21. 論詩三十首（其十九）（元好問）Poems on Poetry Composition (No. 19) (Yuan Haowen)
   因為愛（林明理）Owing to Love (Lin Ming-Li) ………… 68

22. 論詩三十首（其二十二）（元好問）Poems on Poetry Composition (No. 22) (Yuan Haowen)
   黑夜無法將你的光和美拭去（林明理）The Dark Night Fails to Wipe Out Your Beauty and Light (Lin Ming-Li) ………… 70

23. 論詩三十首（其二十四）（元好問）Poems on Poetry Composition (No. 24) (Yuan Haowen)
   行經河深處（林明理）Through Depth of the River (Lin Ming-Li) ……………………………………… 72

24. 杏花雜詩三首（其一）（元好問）Three Poems on Apricot Flowers (No. 1) (Yuan Haowen)
   愛無畏懼（林明理）Love Without Fear (Lin Ming-Li) ……… 74

25. 杏花雜詩三首（其二）（元好問）Three Poems on Apricot Flowers (No. 2) (Yuan Haowen)
   紅櫻樹下（林明理）Under Sakura Trees (Lin Ming-Li) …… 76

26. 杏花雜詩八首（其五）（元好問）Eight Poems on Apricot Flowers (No. 5) (Yuan Haowen)
   思念似雪花緘默地飛翔（林明理）Thoughts Fly Silently Like Snowflakes (Lin Ming-Li) ……………………… 78

27. 遊天壇雜詩（元好問）A Poem on the Heaven Temple Mountain (Yuan Haowen)
   在那山海之間（林明理）Between the Mountains and the Sea (Lin Ming-Li) ……………………………………… 80

28. 京都元夕（元好問）The Lantern Festival in the Capital (Yuan Haowen)
   秋日的港灣（林明理）The Harbor in Autumn (Lin Ming-Li) ‥ 82

29. 梁園春五首（其一）（元好問）Five Poems on a Gardenful of Spring (No. 1) (Yuan Haowen)
   亭溪行（林明理）Strolling Along the Pavilion Creek (Lin Ming-Li) ·················· 83
30. 山居雜詩（其一）（元好問）Miscellaneous Poems About the Mountain Life (No. 1) (Yuan Haowen)
   嵩山之夢（林明理）The Dream of Songshan Mountain (Lin Ming-Li) ·················· 85

▶ 元朝 Yuan Dynasty

31. 題龍陽縣青草湖（唐珙）To the Green Grass Lake (Tang Gong)
   秋暮（林明理）Autumn Dusk (Lin Ming-Li) ·················· 89
32. 觀梅有感（劉因）Inspired by Plum Blossoms (Liu Yin)
   我瞧見…（林明理）I Saw… (Lin Ming-Li) ·················· 90
33. 師師檀板（瞿佑）Li Shishi, a Famous Courtezan-Musician (Qu You)
   影子　灑落愛丁堡上（林明理）The Shadow Is Splashed on Edinburgh (Lin Ming-Li) ·················· 92
34. 過湖口望廬山（方回）Viewing the Lushan Mountain After Crossing the Lake (Fang Hui)
   愛的實現（林明理）The Fulfilment of Love (Lin Ming-Li) ··· 93
35. 客舍雨（熊禾）The Hotel Rain (Xiong He)
   思念似穿過月光的鯨群之歌（林明理）Yearning Is Like the Song of a School of Whales Through the Moonlight (Lin Ming-Li) ·················· 95
36. 題李鶴田穆陵大事記後（劉詵）The Afterword (Liu Shen)
   崖邊的流雲（林明理）Flowing Clouds Over the Cliff (Lin Ming-Li) ·················· 97
37. 題陳渭叟紫雲編（葉森）An Inscription (Ye Sen)
   秋夕（林明理）The Autumn Eve (Lin Ming-Li) ·················· 99
38. 隱居松（張雨）The Hermit-Pine-Tree (Zhang Yu)
   冀望（林明理）Hope (Lin Ming-Li) ·················· 100

39. 絕句（趙孟頫）A Quatrain (Zhao Mengfu)
    讓愛自由（林明理）Let Love Be Free (Lin Ming-Li) ········ 102
40. 絕句（釋英）A Quatrain (Shi Ying)
    二〇〇九年冬天（林明理）The Winter of 2009 (Lin Ming-Li) ·· 103
41. 上京即事（薩都剌）A Hunting Scene (Sa Dula)
    帕德嫩神廟（林明理）The Patrhenon (Lin Ming-Li) ········ 105
42. 過高郵射陽湖（薩都剌）Passing by the Sheyang Lake (Sa Dula)
    寫給科爾多瓦猶太教堂的歌（林明理）A Song for the
    Cordoba Synagogue (Lin Ming-Li) ···················· 107
43. 秋夜聞笛（薩都剌）Fluting in an Autumn Night (Sa Dula)
    笛在深山中（林明理）Fluting in the Deep Mountain
    (Lin Ming-Li) ·· 109
44. 池荷（黃庚）Pond Lotus Blossoms (Huang Geng)
    清雨塘（林明理）The Pond of Limpid Rain (Lin Ming-Li) ··· 111
45. 江村即事（黃庚）A Riverside Village (Huang Geng)
    山間小路（林明理）A Path in the Mountain（Lin Ming-Li）··· 112
46. 暮景（黃庚）A Dusk Scene (Huang Geng)
    在匆匆一瞥間（林明理）A Fleeting Glimpse (Lin Ming-Li) ···· 114
47. 江鄉夜興（尹延高）Night of the Riverside Village (Yin Yengao)
    午夜（林明理）Midnight (Lin Ming-Li) ······················ 116
48. 蓮藕花葉圖（吳師道）On the Painting of Lotus Flowers
    (Wu Shidao)
    富源觀景台冥想（林明理）Meditation on the Fuyuan
    Viewing Platform (Lin Ming-Li) ···························· 117
49. 風雨圖（許衡）A Scene: Winds & Rains (Xu Heng)
    林田山之歌（林明理）Songs of Lintiansan (Lin Ming-Li) ··· 119
50. 登天王台（許衡）Ascending to the Heavenly Platform (Xu Heng)
    淡水紅毛城（林明理）Tamshui Former British Consulate
    (Lin Ming-Li) ·· 120
51. 宿卓水（其一）（許衡）Lodging by the Zhuoshui River
    (No. 1) (Xu Heng)
    遠方傳來的樂音（林明理）Music Wafting From Afar
    (Lin Ming-Li) ·· 124

52. 宿卓水（其二）（許衡）Lodging by the Zhuoshui River (No. 2) (Xu Heng)
夜航（林明理）Night Traveling (Lin Ming-Li) ················ 125

53. 別友人（許衡）Bidding Adieu to a Friend (Xu Heng)
我倆相識絕非偶然（林明理）Our Meeting Is No Coincidence (Lin Ming-Li) ················ 127

54. 城西游（劉秉忠）Touring the West Town (Liu Bingzhong)
黃昏的福州山（林明理）Dusk on the Fuzhou Mountain (Lin Ming-Li) ················ 128

55. 小溪（劉秉忠）A Little Creek (Liu Bingzhong)
沒有一個海域比得上阿曼灣（林明理）There Is No Sea Like the Gulf of Oman (Lin Ming-Li) ················ 130

56. 溪上（劉秉忠）On the Creek (Liu Bingzhong)
春草（林明理）Spring Grass (Lin Ming-Li) ················ 132

57. 三月（劉秉忠）March (Liu Bingzhong)
七月（林明理）July (Lin Ming-Li) ················ 134

58. 畫鴨（揭傒斯）Painting of Ducklings (Jie Xisi)
妳是一條聖光的溪流—致倫札・阿涅利（林明理）You Are a Stream of Sacred Light — to Renza Agnelli (Lin Ming-Li) ···· 136

59. 寒夜作（揭傒斯）Inspired on a Cold Night (Jie Xisi)
可仍記得（林明理）Do You Still Remember (Lin Ming-Li) ··· 138

60. 秋雁（揭傒斯）Migratory Wild Geese (Jie Xisi)
獨白（林明理）Soliloquy (Lin Ming-Li) ················ 140

61. 題信上人春蘭秋蕙二首（其二）（揭傒斯）Two Inscriptions on the Painting by a Monk-Friend (No. 2) (Jie Xisi)
如果（林明理）If (Lin Ming-Li) ················ 142

62. 女兒浦歌二首（其二）（揭傒斯）Two Poems on the Daughter Bay (No. 2) (Jie Xisi)
愛的讚歌（林明理）The Hymn of Love (Lin Ming-Li) ······ 144

63. 雲錦溪棹歌五首（其五）（揭傒斯）Five Boating Songs (No. 5) (Jie Xisi)
   為雨林而歌（林明理）In Praise of the Rain Forest (Lin Ming-Li) ·················146

64. 和歐陽南陽月夜思（揭傒斯）In Reply to Ouyang Nanyang on a Moonlit Night (Jie Xisi)
   從海邊回來（林明理）Back From the Sea (Lin Ming-Li)···148

65. 蘇台竹枝詞（楊維楨）Song of Bamboo Branch (Yang Weizhen)
   靜靜的岱山湖（林明理）The Quiet Daishan Lake (Lin Ming-Li) ···············151

66. 繡（楊維楨）Embroidery (Yang Weizhen)
   簡靜是美（林明理）Quiet Is Beauty (Lin Ming-Li) ··········152

67. 題春江漁父圖（楊維楨）Poem on the Painting (Yang Weizhen)
   冬日湖畔的柔音（林明理）The Soft Music by the Winter Lake (Lin Ming-Li) ·················154

68. 墨梅（王冕）Plum Flowers in Ink (Wang Mian)
   茂林紫蝶幽谷（林明理）Maolin Purple Butterflies Valley (Lin Ming-Li) ·················156

69. 梅花（王冕）Plum Blossoms (Wang Mian)
   武陵農場風情（林明理）Kaleidoscope of Wuling Farm (Lin Ming-Li) ·················158

70. 白梅（王冕）White Plum Blossoms (Wang Mian)
   永懷學者詩人楊牧（林明理）Eternal Memory of Yang Mu As a Poet-Scholar (Lin Ming-Li) ·················160

71. 梅花（其六）（王冕）Plum Blossoms (No. 6) (Wang Mian)
   在思念的夜裡（林明理）In the Night of Longing (Lin Ming-Li) ·················162

72. 過濟源登裴公亭（耶律楚材）Passing Jiyuan and Climbing Peigong Pavilion (Yelü Chucai)
   時光裡的和平島（林明理）The Island of Peace in Time (Lin Ming-Li) ·················164

73. 過天山和上人韻二絕（其一）（耶律楚材）In Reply to a Monk-Friend (No.1) (Yelü Chucai)
山韻（林明理）The Charm of the Mountain (Lin Ming-Li)‧‧167
74. 懷親二首（其二）（耶律楚材）Longing for My Relative (No. 2) (Yelü Chucai)
寒風吹起（林明理）When Cold Wind Blows (Lin Ming-Li)‧‧169
75. 夜坐彈離騷（耶律楚材）Night Sitting & Playing The Parting Sorrow (Yelü Chucai)
流星雨（林明理）The Meteor Shower (Lin Ming-Li)‧‧‧‧‧‧‧‧171
76. 洞山五位頌（耶律楚材）The Field Scenery (Yelü Chucai)
春日的玉山（林明理）The Jade Mountain in Spring (Lin Ming-Li)‧‧‧‧‧‧‧‧‧‧‧‧‧‧‧‧‧‧‧‧‧‧‧‧‧‧‧‧‧‧‧‧‧‧‧‧172
77. 透脫不透脫（耶律楚材）When the Port Is Open to Navigation? (Yelü Chucai)
與菊城開封相會（林明理）Meeting in Kaifeng as a City of Chrysanthemums (Lin Ming-Li)‧‧‧‧‧‧‧‧‧‧‧‧‧‧‧176
78. 三月廿日題所寓屋壁（倪瓚）Inscription on the Wall (Ni Tsan)
寒冬過後（林明理）After the Winter (Lin Ming-Li)‧‧‧‧‧‧‧‧‧177
79. 晚照軒偶題（倪瓚）An Impromtu (Ni Tsan)
默禱（林明理）Silent Prayer (Lin Ming-Li)‧‧‧‧‧‧‧‧‧‧‧‧‧‧‧179
80. 客舍詠牽牛花（倪瓚）The Morning Glory (Ni Tsan)
緬懷山寺之音（林明理）Memory of the Sound of Mountains & Temples (Lin Ming-Li)‧‧‧‧‧‧‧‧‧‧‧‧‧‧‧‧‧‧‧‧‧‧‧‧‧‧‧‧‧‧‧‧‧181
81. 吳仲圭山水（倪瓚）The Landscape of Hills and Rills (Ni Tsan)
重歸自然（林明理）Return to Nature (Lin Ming-Li)‧‧‧‧‧‧‧183
82. 偶成（倪瓚）An Impromptu (Ni Tsan)
妝點秋天（林明理）Spruce Autumn Up (Lin Ming-Li)‧‧‧‧‧185

▶明朝 Ming Dynasty

83. 於郡城送明卿之江西（李攀龍）Parting With a Banished Friend (Li Panlong)
往事（林明理）The Past Events (Lin Ming-Li)‧‧‧‧‧‧‧‧‧‧‧‧‧‧‧‧‧187

84. 登泰山（楊繼盛）Climbing Mount Tai (Yang Jisheng)
又見寒食（林明理）Cold Food Day Again (Lin Ming-Li)‥189
85. 山居夏日（李江）Mountain Living in Summer Days (Li Jiang)
你從太陽裡走來（林明理）You Come Out of the Sun
(Lin Ming-Li) ··191
86. 次韻和王文明絕句漫興十八首（其一）（劉基）Eighteen
Rambling Pieces (No. 1) (Liu Ji)
山茶（林明理）Camellia Flowers (Lin Ming-Li)··············194
87. 夜泉（袁中道）A Night Spring (Yuan Zhongdao)
在秋山的頂上守候（林明理）Keeping Atop the Autumn
Mountain (Lin Ming-Li)··195
88. 次韻和王文明絕句漫興十八首（其五）（劉基）
Eighteen Rambling Pieces (No. 5) (Liu Ji)
懷舊（林明理）Nostalgia (Lin Ming-Li)························197
89. 馬上作（戚繼光）Composed on the Horseback (Qi Jiguang)
回憶的沙漏（林明理）The Hourglass of Memory
(Lin Ming-Li)···199
90. 五月十九日大雨（劉基）Caught in a Heavy Rain (Liu Ji)
雨落在故鄉的泥土上（林明理）The Raindrops Are
Falling in My Hometown (Lin Ming-Li)························200
91. 題沙溪驛（劉基）The Station of Sand & Stream (Liu Ji)
永安鹽田濕地（林明理）The Yongan Wetland (Lin Ming-Li)‥204
92. 春蠶（劉基）Spring Silkworm (Liu Ji)
水蓮（林明理）Water Lilies (Lin Ming-Li)····················207
93. 天平山中（楊基）In the Heaven-Flat Mountain (Yang Ji)
坐覺（林明理）Sitting Sensation (Lin Ming-Li)················208
94. 玉蘭（睢石）Magnolia Flowers (Sui Shi)
魯花樹（林明理）The Tree of Scolopia Oldhamii (Lin Ming-Li)‥211
95. 寄跡武塘賦之（夏完淳）Lodging in Wutang (Xia Wanchun)
你的呼喚—to 普希金 Aleksandr Pushkin（1799-1837）
（林明理）Your Calling — To Aleksandr Pushkin (1799-1837)
(Lin Ming-Li) ···213

96. 題葡萄圖（徐渭）Inscription on a Painting of Grapes (Xu Wei)
    眼睛深處（林明理）Deep in the Eye (Lin Ming-Li) ········ 214
97. 龕山凱歌（徐渭）A Triumphant Song in Kanshan Mountain (Xu Wei)
    佛羅里達山獅（林明理）Florida Panther (Lin Ming-Li) ··· 216
98. 風鳶圖詩（徐渭）Flying the Kite (Xu Wei)
    巴巴里獅（林明理）Panthera Leo Leo (Lin Ming-Li) ······· 218
99. 王元章倒枝梅畫（徐渭）A Painting of Sprawling Plum Flowers (Xu Wei)
    大雪山風景（林明理）The Scenery of the Daxue Mountain (Lin Ming-Li) ·· 220
100. 天河（徐渭）The Heavenly River (Xu Wei)
    在北極荒野中（林明理）In the Arctic Wilderness (Lin Ming-Li) ··· 222
101. 葡萄（徐渭）Grapes (Xu Wei)
    你的榮光──給 prof. Ernesto Kahan（林明理）
    Your Glory— To Professor Ernesto Kahan (Lin Ming-Li) ····· 225
102. 石灰吟（于謙）The Limestone (Yu Qian)
    信天翁（林明理）The Albatross (Lin Ming-Li) ············· 226
103. 除夜太原寒甚（于謙）The Cold New Year's Eve in Taiyuan (Yu Qian)
    夢見中國（林明理）Dreaming of China (Lin Ming-Li) ···· 229
104. 上太行山（于謙）Climbing the Taihang Mountain (Yu Qian)
    它的名字叫山陀兒（林明理）Its Name is Shantar (Lin Ming-Li) ·· 231
105. 絕筆（唐寅）The Last Words (Tang Yin)
    如風往事（林明理）Gone With the Wind (Lin Ming-Li) ·· 233
106. 奉寄孫思和（唐寅）To My Friend Sun Sihe (Tang Yin)
    致珍古德博士（林明理）To Dr. Jane Goodall (Lin Ming-Li) ·· 235
107. 壽王少傅守溪（唐寅）Keeping and Watching the Creek (Tang Yin)
    平靜的湖面（林明理）The Calm Lake (Lin Ming-Li) ····· 236

108. 言志（唐寅）My Ambition (Tang Yin)
路（林明理）The Road (Lin Ming-Li)·····························237
109. 口號三首（其一）（祝允明）Three Impromptu Poems (No. 1) (Zhu Yunming)
父親的手（林明理）Father's Hands (Lin Ming-Li) ········239
110. 夏口夜泊別友人（李夢陽）Parting With a Friend (Zhu Yunming)
我將獨行（林明理）I Will Walk Alone (Lin Ming-Li)······240
111. 汴中元夕五首（其一）（李夢陽）Five Poems About the Lantern Festival in Kaifeng (No. 1) (Li Mengyang)
Love is…（林明理）Love is… (Lin Ming-Li)···············242
112. 汴中元夕五首（其二）（李夢陽）Five Poems About the Lantern Festival in Kaifeng (No. 2) (Li Mengyang)
北風（林明理）The North Wind (Lin Ming-Li)··············244
113. 汴中元夕五首（其三）（李夢陽）Five Poems About the Lantern Festival in Kaifeng (No. 3) (Li Mengyang)
愛的箴言（林明理）The Proverb of Love (Lin Ming-Li)··246
114. 汴中元夕五首（其四）（李夢陽）Five Poems About the Lantern Festival in Kaifeng (No. 4) (Li Mengyang)
寫給包公故里──肥東（林明理）To Bao Gong's Hometown — Feidong (Lin Ming-Li)·······················248
115. 汴中元夕五首（其五）（李夢陽）Five Poems About the Lantern Festival in Kaifeng (No. 5) (Li Mengyang)
你的微笑（林明理）Your Smile (Lin Ming-Li)··············250
116. 重贈吳國賓（邊貢）Parting From a Close Friend (Bian Gong)
請允許我分享純粹的喜悅（林明理）Please Allow Me to Share the Pure Joy (Lin Ming-Li)························251
117. 題美人（邊貢）To a Beauty (Bian Gong)
倒影（林明理）The Inverted Image (Lin Ming-Li)··········253
118. 送蕭若愚（邊貢）Seeing My Friend Off (Bian Gong)
在愉悅夏夜的深邃處（林明理）In the Depth of a Pleasant Summer Night (Lin Ming-Li)·······························254

119. 題畫（沈周）Inscription on a Painting (Shen Zhou)
   西子灣夕照（林明理）The Sunset at Sizihwan
   (Lin Ming-Li) ·· 256
120. 秋閨（謝榛）The Autumn Boudoir (Xie Zhen)
   我如何能夠⋯（林明理）How Can I⋯ (Lin Ming-Li) ⋯258
121. 春日雜詠（高珩）Inspired in Spring (Gao Heng)
   當黎明時分（林明理）At Dawn (Lin Ming-Li) ············259
122. 詠竹（朱元璋）Ode to the Bamboo (Zhu Yuanzhang)
   山野的蝴蝶（林明理）The Mountain Butterflies
   (Lin Ming-Li) ·· 261
123. 東風（朱元璋）The East Wind (Zhu Yuanzhang)
   夏荷（林明理）Summer Lotus (Lin Ming-Li) ················ 262
124. 新雨水（朱元璋）Fresh Rain (Zhu Yuanzhang)
   雨影（林明理）The Shadow of Rain (Lin Ming-Li) ········264
125. 金雞報曉（朱元璋）The Crow of the Rooster as Harbinger
   of Dawn (Zhu Yuanzhang)
   走在砂卡礑步道上（林明理）Walking Along the
   Shakadang Trail (Lin Ming-Li) ·· 266
126. 無題（朱元璋）Without a Title (Zhu Yuanzhang)
   大貓熊（林明理）The Giant Panda (Lin Ming-Li) ············269
127. 罵文士（朱元璋）To Curse the Literary Men
   (Zhu Yuanzhang)
   一則警訊（林明理）A Warning Sign (Lin Ming-Li) ········270
128. 詠菊（朱元璋）To Chrysanthemums (Zhu Yuanzhang)
   東華大學校園印象（林明理）Impression of the Campus
   of Donghua University (Lin Ming-Li) ································ 272
129. 無題（朱元璋）Without a Title (Zhu Yuanzhang)
   洪患（林明理）Flooding (Lin Ming-Li) ···························274
130. 拜年（文徵明）Pay a New Year Call (Wen Zhengming)
   為義大利詩壇樹起了一面精神昂揚的旗幟——寫給
   《PEACE》詩集（林明理）Raising a High-Spirited
   Banner of the Italian Poetry Circle— For the Poetry
   Collection Entitled *PEACE* (Lin Ming-Li) ······················ 275

131. 夜宿瀘山（楊慎）Lodging in Lushan Mountain (Yang Shen)
大安溪夜色（林明理）Da-an River At Night (Lin Ming-Li)⋯277
132. 尋胡隱君（高啟）In Search of a Recluse (Gao Qi)
永懷文學大師——余光中（林明理）Eternal Memory of Yu Guangzhong as a Master of Literature (Lin Ming-Li)⋯⋯⋯279
133. 田舍夜舂（高啟）Husking Rice in the Night (Gao Qi)
原野之聲（林明理）The Sound of the Wilderness (Lin Ming-Li)⋯⋯⋯⋯⋯⋯⋯⋯⋯⋯⋯⋯⋯⋯⋯⋯281
134. 宮女圖（高啟）Painting of a Maid-in-Waiting (Gao Qi)
金山寺的陽光溢滿樹梢（林明理）The Sunshine of Jinshan Temple Fills the Treetops (Lin Ming-Li)⋯⋯⋯282
135. 龍州（林弼）Longzhou (Lin Bi)
悼土耳其強震（林明理）Mourning the Great Earthquake in Turkey (Lin Ming-Li)⋯⋯⋯⋯⋯⋯⋯⋯⋯⋯⋯⋯284
136. 談詩五首（其一）（方孝孺）Five Poems on Poetry Writing (No. 1) (Fang Xiaoru)
老師，請不要忘記我的名（林明理）Dear Teacher, Please Don't Forget My Name (Lin Ming-Li)⋯⋯⋯⋯⋯⋯287
137. 談詩五首（其二）（方孝孺）Five Poems on Poetry Writing (No. 2) (Fang Xiaoru)
邵武戀歌（林明理）Shaowu Love Song (Lin Ming-Li)⋯⋯290
138. 清明有感（楊士奇）Inspired at the Tomb-sweeping Festival (Yang Shiqi)
獻給敘利亞罹難的女童（林明理）Dedicated to the Girls Killed in Syria (Lin Ming-Li)⋯⋯⋯⋯⋯⋯⋯⋯⋯292
139. 劉伯川席上作（楊士奇）Composed at the Banquet of Liu Bochuan (Yang Shiqi)
給普希金 Aleksandr Pushkin（林明理）To Aleksandr Pushkin (Lin Ming-Li)⋯⋯⋯⋯⋯⋯⋯⋯⋯⋯⋯⋯⋯294
140. 揚州（曾棨）Yangzhou (Zeng Qi)
在高原之巔，心是如水的琴弦（林明理）Atop the Plateau, My Heart Is Like the Water-Like Strings (Lin Ming-Li)⋯⋯⋯295

141. 柯敬仲墨竹（李東陽）An Ink Painting of Bamboo
(Li Dongyang)
老橡樹（林明理）An Old Oak (Lin Ming-Li) ·················297
142. 梅花（寧王翠妃）Plum Blossoms (Ning Wang Cuifei)
野桐（林明理）The Wild Parasol Trees (Lin Ming-Li) ········299
143. 頌任公詩（其四）（歸有光）Ode to Ren Huan (No.4)
(Gui Youguang)
朋友（林明理）Friends (Lin Ming-Li) ·······················301
144. 凱歌（沈明臣）A Battle Song (Shen Mingchen)
企鵝的悲歌（林明理）The Dirge of the Penguin
(Lin Ming-Li) ···302
145. 蕭臯別業竹枝詞（沈明臣）A Bamboo Branch Song
(Shen Mingchen)
寫給曹植之歌（組詩）（林明理）A Song for Cao Zhi
(group poems) (Lin Ming-Li) ·······································303
146. 送妻弟魏生還里（王世貞）Sending My Wife's Brother
Back Home (Wang Shizhen)
寫給鞏義之歌──致鞏義市（林明理）A Song for
Gongyi — Dedicated to the City of Gongyi (Lin Ming-Li) ·····306
147. 戚將軍贈寶劍歌二首（其二）（王世貞）Two Poems About
a Treasured Sword (No. 2) (Wang Shizhen)
丁方教授和他的油畫（林明理）Professor Ding Fang and
His Oil Paintings (Lin Ming-Li) ···································308
148. 老病始蘇（李贄）Recovery From a Chronic Disease
(Li Zhi)
短詩一束（林明理）A Group of Short Poems
(Lin Ming-Li) ···310
149. 聞都城渴雨時苦攤稅（湯顯祖）Taxation in Spite of a
Drought (Tang Xianzu)
蝴蝶谷的晨歌（林明理）The Morning Song of Butterfly
Valley (Lin Ming-Li) ···312

25

150. 七夕醉答君東（湯顯祖）Drunk at Double Seventh Festival (Tang Xianzu)
北國的白樺──致謝冕教授（林明理）A White Birch in the Northern Land— to Professor Xie Mian (Lin Ming-Li) ·····315

附錄：夜讀蔡輝振詩集《思無邪》（林明理）
Appendix: Night Reading *Innocent Thinking*, a Poetry Collection by Tsai Huei-Ching（Article and photo by Lin Ming-Li）················317

元詩明理接千載

古今抒情詩三百首

漢英對照

金朝 Jin Dynasty

1・

雞鳴山下橋　　　　　　　　　　趙秉文

兩山相對翠屏開,一水中流礙石回。
橋北橋南路分處,紅塵一騎日邊來。

A Bridge Under the Cockcrow Mountain
Zhao Bingwen

Facing each other, two mountains
exhibit their own emerald screens,

amidst which a river undergoes a
reversed flow against huge rocks.

A fork in the road, north and south
of the bridge, welcomes a rider on

the horse running from the sun-side
through wreaths of rolling red dust.

山楂樹　　　　　　　　　　　　林明理

我在暮色中網住一只鳥
牠有秋月般的暈黃
虹彩般的髮
我願意朝夕地守望
每當牠迅速地
驕矜地

把一個白霜的山丘
圈在牠的腳踝上

春神在我臂下休息
仲夜從我身邊溜去
我沿著小路沒有回頭
直想輕步接近牠的孤獨身軀
冬風不停地呼嘯而去
但我只能前行
直到牠帶回長長的回音：
呵，忘卻你，忘卻我……

——是動中無聲的安寧

Hawthorn Tree Lin Ming-Li

In the twilight I have netted a bird
Its fluffy yellow is like the autumn moon
Its feather is the color of rainbow
I would rather keep watching it day and night
Each time it suddenly
And proudly
Ties the hoarfrost- covered hill
To its paws

The goddess of spring rests under my arms
Midnight glides away by my side
I walk along the path without looking back
Only think of approaching its lonely stature
Winter whistling and howling and passing
Until it brings back the long echoing
Ah, forget you, and forget me ....

— It is the silent peace in motion

元詩明理楼千載
古今抒情詩三百首
漢英對照

2.

溪行   李庭

枯木扶疏夾道傍，野梅倒影浸寒塘。
朝陽不到溪灣處，留得橫橋一板霜。

Strolling Along the Creek   Li Ting

The road is choked with withered
trees after mouldering woods;

the cold pond is invaded by the
reflection of wild plum blossoms.

The morning sun fails to reach
the bend of the creek, where

a plank bridge is filmed
with frost: clean and intact.

淡水紅毛城之歌   林明理

1.
我總愛在深夜，開始傾聽。你在
冬天黎明的嘆息。

2.
啊，寂寞的城。
你載著往日的歷史和明天的月光，

雙眼輕閉著，歌裡永遠縈繞著一條母親的河；
它總是那麼平靜——平靜地，
被風帶往大海的懷抱。

3.
你就像詩曲，擁有一切的悲傷和歡樂。
你留在我眼底的雙眸，深邃而遺世。

4.
露台的槍眼已成過眼雲煙，
故鄉的圓月永遠不會衰老；
然後，隱隱聽見，
觀音的微笑慢慢綻開，綿延成島嶼之花。

5.
我聽見了草坪鏽砲上的歌聲，歌聲跳盪在
冬天的童話裡，來回尋找失落的故事。

6.
啊，我總愛在深夜，才開始傾聽；
你的歌聲——在流年的河裡，
隨著月輝的照耀，讓人感到溫暖而幸福。

Fortress San Domingo, Song of Danshui
                                        Lin Ming-Li

1.
I always love to, in the depth of night, start listening. You are
Sighing at the dawn of winter.

2.
Ah, lonely city.
You carry the history of yore and the moonlight of tomorrow,
Two eyes gently closed, the song is forever lingering with a motherly river;

It is always so quiet — quietly,
Carried away to bosom of the sea by wind.

3.
You are like a poem, which is filled with all joys and sorrows.
The eyes which you leave in my eyes are deep, detached from the world.

4.
The loophole on the terrace has been transient as a fleeting cloud,
The hometown moon will never age;
Then, it is faintly hearable,
The smile of Kwan-yin slowly blossoms, spreading into flowers on the island.

5.
I have heard a song from the rusty artillery gun on the turf, which is bouncing
In winter fairy tales, looking back and forth for lost stories.

6.
Ah, I always love to, in the depth of night, start listening;
Your song — in the river of the running year,
With the shining of the moonlight, we feel warm and happy.

❋ ❋ ❋

3·

絕句 王庭筠

竹影和詩瘦，梅花入夢香。
可憐今夜月，不肯下西廂。

A Quatrain

Wang Tingjun

The bamboo shadows, clean and clear, are in harmony with poetry;

the scented plum blossoms enter my fond dream. Loveable is the

moon tonight, which is reluctant to fall from the west-wing room.

想妳，在墾丁

林明理

每年落山風吹起
是墾丁旅遊的淡季
但我總會想起妳
如同孤鳥
整夜不眠地徘徊在
月光覆蓋的礁岩上

當我拾起貝殼，貼進耳裡
我就感到驚奇，彷彿
那座軍艦石潛過大海
瞧，妳長髮如樹冠的葉片般
柔美而飄逸
瞬間，如夏雨

蘇鐵睡眠著、白野花兒睡眠著
甚至連星兒也那樣熟睡了
只有沉默的島嶼對我們說話──
就讓時間蒼老吧
這世界已有太多東西逝去
我只想擁有自然、夜，和珍貴的友誼

元詩明理撼千載
古今抒情詩三百首
漢英對照

I Miss You, in Kending   Lin Ming-Li

Each year when the northern-east wind blows
It is the slack season for traveling in Kending
But I never fail to remember you
Like a lonely bird
Which lingers on the reef bright with
moonlight through the sleepless night

When I pick up a shell and put it to my ears
I always feel the wonder, as if
That rock of warship has moved across the sea
Lo, your long hair is like the tree leaves
Which is fair, elegant and beautiful
In a blink, it is like a summer shower

Cycad trees are asleep, and wild white flowers are asleep
Even the stars are also sound asleep
Only the silent island talks to us —
Let time age and old
Too many things in the world have disappeared
I only want to possess the nature, night, and valuab

4.

嗅梅圖   李仲略

朧朧霽色冷黃昏，缺月疏籬水外村。
人在天涯花在手，一枝香雪寄銷魂。

The Picture of Smelling Plum Flowers
Li Zhonglüe

Letup of a rainfall, the dusk is
cold and hazy; a waning moon

over the sparse fence shines over
a village beyond the river. From

a wanderer in the horizon, a bunch
of flowers in her hand; whispers of

love through a snowy spray shaggy
with lingering missing & yearning.

在我窗前起舞
林明理

和風歇在桂花樹梢
窗外滿是絨毯兒
每一片
都似柳絮的輕柔

當黃昏的淡雲飄來
你便在我的眼底隱逝了……那時
冬原正是一片空曠，將慢慢，更慢地
透出明亮嚴肅的冷光——

Dancing in Front of My Window
Lin Ming-Li

A gentle breeze rests atop the tree of may flowers
Without the window it is all velvety carpet
Each piece
Is like the tenderness of willow catkins

When the pale clouds of dusk waft here
You fade out from the bottom of my eyes　then
The winter field is all blankness, slowly, more slowly
To reveal a solemn cold beam of light —

🌱 🌱 🌱

5 ·

不出　　　　　　　　　　　　　　　　　　劉仲尹

好詩讀罷倚團蒲，唧唧銅瓶沸地爐。
天氣稍寒吾不出，氍毹分坐與狸奴。

To Stay Home　　　　　　　　　　　　Liu Zhongyin

Reading good poems,
I lean against a round

cattail mat, when the copper
kettle on the pit furnace

is boiling and sizzling. It
being cold outside, I stay

home, sitting, with my pet
cat, on the patterned carpet.

那年冬夜　　　　　　　　　　　　　　　　林明理

你的憂懼巨大
而蜷伏

我的恰似
月下草上失足的孤星

生命
正從身邊溜過
什麼時候我重生
哪裡是我夢中的雲影

我們的記憶
是淺鑄的
一面
淚鏡

That Winter Night　　　　　　Lin Ming-Li

With a deep sorrow
You coil up
Like my lonely star
On the grass under the moon with a false move

Life
Is slipping by me
When am I to be reborn
Where is the cloudy shadow in my dream

Our memory
Is a teary
Mirror
Of shallow cast

6.

自理 　　　　　　　　　　　　　　　　　劉仲尹

日日南軒學蠹魚，隱中獨愛隱於書。
兒癡婦笑謀生拙，不道從來與世疏。

Self-help 　　　　　　　　　　　　　Liu Zhongyin

Beneath the southern window
I am a follower of the book-

worm, who, from day to day,
loves to seclude itself in a book.

Children and women laugh at
me for my clumsiness in making

a living, without knowing that
I am a stranger to worldly ways.

我的夢想 　　　　　　　　　　　　　　　林明理

所有在我想像世界裡的詩
都變化於更寬廣之心的轉驛站
無論是幻想或夢境
或有多少不可能要驅馳
我相信生命是圓的
在孤獨之中仍有真正的友誼
分享彼此的快樂與苦痛

My Dream

Lin Ming-Li

All the poems in the world of my imagination
Have changed into the station of a broader heart
Be it a fantasy or a dream
Or how much impossibility in galloping and driving forward
My belief is that life is round
Genuine friendship in loneliness
To share each other's joys and pain

❀ ❀ ❀

7 ·

寒夜

劉仲尹

漏聲穿竹夜霜清，盡著功夫伴短檠。
睡足梅花半梢月，虛徐老鼻學香生。

The Cold Night

Liu Zhongyin

The ticktock of hourglass travels
through the grove of bamboos veiled

in night frost clean and clear, when
a short lamp is spent in close reading

through patient efforts. Plum blossoms,
awake from their slumbering, admire

half a disc of moon; there is sniffing
of their sweet scent, in a slow swirl⋯

綠淵潭   林明理

若沒了這群山脈,恐怕妳將分不清
通向另一片蔚藍的希望之船,
那裏黎明正在沾滿白雪的雲階上等妳。

總是,在分別的時刻才猛然想起
潭邊小屋恬靜地下著棋,當晚星
把妳從落了葉的岳樺樹後帶往我身邊,
別憂懼,我已沿著那隱蔽的淒清昏光
滑入閃爍的冰叢外虛寂的海洋。

Green Deep Pond   Lin Ming-Li

Without the mountain ranges, it is hard for you to distinguish
The ship of hope sailing to another blue sea,
Where the dawn is waiting for you on the cloudy stairs covered with snow.

Always, a sudden thought upon parting
Quietly playing chess in the pond-side cottage, when evening star
Brings you to me from behind the leafless birch,
No worry, along the dreary faint light from the shady spot,
I have slipped into the empty ocean beyond the glittering ice.

8 ·

初秋夜涼 劉仲尹

小蟲機杼月西廂，風雨才分半枕涼。
白髮自疏河漢夢，一瓶秋水玉簪香。

The Cold Night of Early Autumn
Liu Zhongyin

Insects are vociferous until the
loom in the room, a moon over

the western chamber; the wind
& rain bring cool and cold to half

a pillow. Gray hairs are thinning
by themselves, a fond dream of

the Silver River; a bottle of autumn
water, a scented jade hair stick.

星河 林明理

你是否來自那不變的七星潭
夜這般空明，草海桐目光澹澹
八月，波賽頓啊，讓林投之雀
在那聽雨於空谷的棲地
在那北岸的砂原後方
為黑潮的子民輕唱
有誰記得海階或碧崖

望盡雲路的傷感
任憑你來時如風浩浩
歸去又怎堪笑對故鄉

The River of Stars Lin Ming-Li

Are you from the constant Seven Star Lake
The night is so empty-bright, the eyes of scaevola are limpid
August, oh, Poseidon, for the forest-bound sparrows
In the habitat of listening to rain in the empty valley
Behind the sandy plain of the northern bank
To gently sing for the descendants of the Black Tide
Who remembers the coastal terrace or the green cliff
To exhaustively watch the sentimentality of the cloudy road
Despite your coming like a spell of wind
Returning, how to face your hometown with a smile

9.

夏日 劉仲尹

床頭書冊聚麻沙,病起經旬不煮茶。
更為炎蒸設方略,細烹山蜜破松花。

The Summer Day Liu Zhongyin

The head of my bed is
infested with books of

poor quality; diseased
for ten days, no tea is

brewed. Resourceful
against the scorching heat:

mountain honey & pine
flowers are carefully boiled.

夏日慵懶的午後　　　　　　　　林明理

有座被鳥雀和
蓮花簇擁的小森林，
湖面似透鏡，
雲終於落下來。
我踮起腳尖，
按下快門的一瞬，
細碎的陽光是背景，
天空無語，卻令我沉迷。
我以為自己可以及時
找到真理和歡樂，
那遺世的孤獨
已離開很遠；
風總是靜靜地吹，
在這夏日慵懶的午後。

A Languid Summer Afternoon
　　　　　　　　　　　　Lin Ming-Li

There is a little forest,
Surrounded by birds and lotus flowers;
The lake surface is like a mirror
Upon which clouds finally fall.

I stand on tiptoe,
And when I press the shutter of my camera,
The fragmented sunlight as the background,
I am enthralled by the wordless sky.
I believe I can find truth
And happiness in time,
When the loneliness of the world
Has been far away.
The wind is always blowing gently,
In the languid summer afternoon.

10 ·

一室 　　　　　　　　　　　　　　　　劉仲尹

老來湖海愧陳登，只有頭須未是僧。
坐對黃昏鐘鼓定，竹根吹火上吟燈。

A Solitary Room　　　　　　　　Liu Zhongyin

In my advanced age, I lack
the code of brotherhood of

Chen Deng, and my head
does not assume that of

a monk. Sitting in dusk,
enveloped in the sound of

drums & bells; bamboo roots
as firewood, a lamp is reading.

林中小徑的黃昏　　　　　　　　林明理

層層枯葉
篩落著你四季的足音。

就像扇動北風的羊鈴,
你在眾神的沉默中漫過,

霧像宿鳥般
將夢之翼繫在歌瀑上。
棲身在石壁的雲杉,
深藏著你的思想。

而那飄閃的浪花
輕輕把回憶安放,
它教會我
敲下那空洞的希望。

在靜寂中雪泥輝耀,
這雲杉彷彿一起飛揚。

The Dusk of a Path in the Forest
　　　　　　　　　　　　Lin Ming-Li

Layers of withered leaves
To screen your footfalls through the four seasons.

Like the sheep bell fanning the north wind,
Slowly you spill over in the silence of all deities,

The fog, like nesting birds,
Ties the dreamy wings to the waterfall of the songs.

The spruce trees which hide themselves against the stony walls,
With your thought hidden in the depth.

The flickering waves
Settle the memory gently;
It teaches me
To knock at the empty hope.

In silence muddy snow shines brilliant,
As if the spruce trees are flying together.

11 ·

二月十一日見桃花　　　　　　　　高士談

鳴鳩天色半晴陰，竹屋松窗老寸心。
閉戶不知春早晚，桃花紅淺柳青深。

At the First Sight of Peach Flowers
Gao Shitan

Turtledoves are cooing in the
air half cloudy and half sunny;

the bamboo house & the pine
window and an inch of old

heart. A closed door knows
not the spring: thriving? Or

fading? Peach flowers are pale
red, and willows: deep green.

布拉格猶太人墓園[1]

林明理

我在福爾摩莎聽到
　一支遠方的歌
一批古老的靈魂流浪著
　由一國到另一國
　直到他們找到這個地方
　可以讓他們平靜地安息了
我輕輕地
　收集你們的淚水
　擲給月光的輝耀
並在每一墓碑上……
　　　……外加一塊石

The Jewish Cemetery in Prague[2]

Lin Ming-Li

In Formosa, I hear
　A distant song
A group of old souls are wandering
　From a country to another country
　Until they find this place
　For them to settle and rest
I gently
　Collect your tears
　The brilliant moonlight thrown to the moon

---

[1] 老猶太公墓（Starý židovský hřbitov）位於捷克首都布拉格，自 15 世紀初開始使用，直至 1787 年。據估計，目前發現大約有 12,000 個墓碑，可能有多達 10 萬人的墓葬。

[2] Located in the Czech capital Prague, the old Jewish Cemetery (Starý židovský hřbitov) was in use from the beginning of the 15th century until 1787. It is estimated that there are currently about 12,000 tombstones, which may have buried one hundred thousand people.

And on each and every tombstone
⋯I place an extra stone

❦ ❦ ❦

12 ·

楊花 高士談

來時宮柳萬絲黃,去日飛球滿路旁。
我比楊花更飄蕩,楊花只是一春忙。

Willow Filaments Gao Shitan

Coming, myriads of slender
palace willow twigs are on the

yellowing; leaving, the road is
rolling with downy balls on the

balling. Poplar filaments are flitting
and flying through a spring, when

I, as a rover, am roving through
a lifetime of one hundred springs.

流蘇花開[3] 林明理

一隻自由翩翩的歌雀
周圍是切割千面的翡翠

---

[3] 每次到臺大校園看到流蘇花開,都情不自禁癡迷於它的美!再一次信步來到它跟前,只想為它表白心跡。

像片片溫暖的雪
淡淡的
輕拂
四月的雲天
風仍傳頌著
你的名和那些你喜愛的
紅杜鵑
在初夏微風的醉月湖
夜鴉拍綠了水畔
你的歌聲鳴囀，蕩漾
直等到移開我的視線
噢，我的雪雀
你是聖潔的詩人
輝耀在巍巍學府間

Tassel Flowering[4]   Lin Ming-Li

A sparrow of free flying
All about is the emerald to cut all faces
Like a flake after another warm flake
Gently and slightly
To kiss away
The cloudy sky of April
The wind is still spreading
Your name and the red azalea
Which you like best
Over the drunken moon lake under the gentle wind of the beginning summer

---

[4] Each time at the sight of the tassel flowering at Taiwan University, I am infatuated with its beauty. Now once more approaching it, I cannot help expressing my heartfelt fond wishes for it.

Night owls have flapped green the water
Your singing is melodious, rippling
Until my vision is diverted
Oh, my snow finch
You are a holy and pure poet
Brilliant in the grand seats of learning

13 ·

雪 高士談

蔌蔌天花落未休，寒梅疏竹共風流。
江山一色三千里，酒力消時正倚樓。

Snow Gao Shitan

Heavenly flowers are falling showers
upon showers — the spectacle is

adorned with cold plum blossoms
& sparse bamboos. Hills and rills

are one color, stretching for myriads
of miles; the effects of alcohol

dispelled, the drinker is leaning
against the balustrade of the mansion.

夜讀《帶著愛去斯基亞索斯島 TO SKIATHOS WITH LOVE》[5]

林明理

1.
我不必引頸翹望,
斯基亞索斯島的天空
本來就是諸神的殿堂。

2.
它是月亮的偏愛,
對詩人來說,
是可天天吟詠的臉龐。

3.
它是愛琴海的琴師,
有著永恆的,無法抹滅的,
或緊繫遊子們的名字。

4.
它口吐大海的氣味,
更勝過世上任何馨香…
在島嶼和天地之間。

5.
人們習慣於它純藍的自由,

---

[5] 今年二月間,由義大利詩人 Giovanni Campisi 與其他兩位希臘詩人瑪麗亞·卡拉齊(Maria Kalatzi)、斯特拉·萊昂蒂亞杜(Stella Leontiadou)一起在義大利出版一本圖文並茂的詩集《帶著愛去斯基亞索斯島 TO SKIATHOS WITH LOVE》,內容有的是頌揚希臘最北端的一座純淨而獨特的小島,位於愛琴海西北部;有的是關注希臘在早年 1770 年至 1821 年的片斷歷史,引入遐思。我在降臨的夜色中閱讀後,詩集中的有些詩句在腦海中迴轉,給我送來了靈思,遂而寫下此詩。

即使歷史重來，
也篤定會被世人所珍愛。

——2024.02.14 寫於臺灣

Night reading *TO SKIATHOS WITH LOVE*[6]

Lin Ming-Li

1.
I don't have to crane my neck to look up,
The sky of Skiathos
It is originally the temple of gods.

2.
It is the favor of the moon,
For the poets,
It is a face that can be chanted every day.

3.
It is the pianist of the Aegean Sea,
With a permanent, indelible,
Or closely tied to the names of the wanderers.

4.
It breathes the smell of the sea,
Better than any fragrance in the world...
Between islands and heaven and earth.

---

[6] In February, 2024, Italian poet Giovanni Campisi and Greek poets Maria Kalatzi and Stella Leontiadou, together published a book of pictures and texts in Italy. The collection of poems TO SKIATHOS WITH LOVE contains some eulogizing of a pure and unique island in the northernmost part of Greece, which is located in the northwest Aegean Sea; some focus on Greece's early years from 1770 to 1821. The fragmented history of the years stirred my reverie. Reading it in the falling night, some of the poems in the collection inspired me to write this poem.

5.
People are accustomed to its pure blue freedom,
Even if history repeats itself,
It is sure to be cherished by the world.

    Written in Taiwan on February 14, 2024

14 ·

睡起   高士談

平生心性樂疏慵，多病追歡興亦空。
睡起不知春已老，一簾紅雨杏花風。

Awake From a Sleep   Gao Shitan

Lazy and loose in nature, I
am a reveler, in spite of my

disease, reveling in joys and
pleasures. Awake from a sleep,

I know not spring is on the
waning, to be old: a curtainful

of red shower slightly blown
in the wind of apricot flowers.

加路蘭[7]的晨歌

林明理

在朵朵浪花和歌聲間
我的詩琴撥弄著。我喜愛它
遠甚於那些瑰麗的岩貌，
只要時間緩緩停泊於
曙光中珊瑚謳歌的所在，
或將喜悅傳遞給群山，
還有落葉與鳴蟲。

它是如此純淨，寬廣而不羈，
比想像中還要真實——
美麗千倍的美景。
有月懸在雲間，
有風笛吹起相思…
而遠方冉冉升起的太陽
是我浮出的燦然的笑。

The Morning Song of Garulan[8]

Lin Ming-Li

Amidst waves and songs
My poetry-lute is playing. I love it
Far better than the rosy rocky appearance,
So long as time slowly stops
At the spot of coral songs bathed in the dawning light,

---

[7] 「加路蘭」原為臺東空軍建設志航基地機場時的廢棄土置場，經多次規劃並以生態工法開發後，如今已成為美麗的休憩區。

[8] Garulan is a disused soil disposal yard from the original construction of Chi-hang Base Airport by Taitung Air Force which, through renovations and development, is now a beautiful scenic spot.

Or the joy is delivered to the mountains,
As well as falling leaves and chirping insects.

It is so pure, wide and unrestrained,
More real than imagination —
The beautiful scenery which is beauty itself.
The moon is hanging in the clouds;
The bagpipe is piping pining and yearning…
The sun is slowly rising from afar
Which is my beaming smile floating up.

🍀 🍀 🍀

15 ·

道中 高士談

鳴鳩逐婦婦欲去，燕子引雛雛不來。
樹底樹頭千點雨，山南山北一聲雷。

En Route Gao Shitan

Turtledoves run after a woman who
is on the point of leaving; swallows

nurture fledglings who refuse to be
followers. The bottom and the top

of the tree are noisy with thousands
of raindrops; the northern mountains

and the southern mountains are
shivering with a peal of thunder.

愛是一種光亮　　　　　　　　　　林明理

遺失在黑洞內的音訊：
縱使是宇宙微塵的一部份
但我們之間卻是註定的孤獨。

彷彿夜空舞臺的新星，一晃即逝
如孢子散於花瓣。
我們無法停止的每一脈動
將在彼此凝視中放射於
淡淡的雲層
儘管我們距離隔橫。

驀然回首
我站立赤道的某一角落
循著逆時鐘方向
旋轉，不管秋分至春分
是否畫短夜長？

愛，是一種光亮。

Love Is a Kind of Light　　　　　Lin Ming-Li

The message lost in the black hole:
Although a portion of the tiny dust of the universe,
There is doomed loneliness between us.

Like a new star on the stage of the night sky, flashing and
vanishing,

Like spores being scattered on the petals.
Each throb of the pulse which we fail to stop,
Will radiate through mutual gaze from each other,
Radiating from the pale clouds,
In spite of the distance between us.

Suddenly to look back,
I stand at a corner of the equator,
In counterclockwise direction;
Turning, from autumnal equinox to spring equinox,
Careless of the short days or long nights.

Love is a kind of light.

🌿 🌿 🌿

16 ·

偶題　　　　　　　　　　　　　　高士談

羨他田父老于農，遠是莊西與舍東。
不似宦遊情味惡，半生常在別離中。

An Impromptu Piece　　　Gao Shitan

Enviable: the field-tilling farmers
in the same village are as far

as the west end and the east end,
while, to seek official posts,

the seekers, for half a lifetime,
are seeking high and low, going

from place to place — on the
going, and on the leaving…

那年冬天 　　　　　　　　　　　　　　　　　林明理

小心翼翼
翻開
一張張塵封已久
藏在箱櫃底的照片
仍渾樸的
展露一滴一滴的古趣

當年歲
西移
春的迷醉還未甦醒
石階上枯葉窸窣
杏花兒又長滿了新綠
風，在嬉鬧中穿梭如蝶

而我
將停頓的思緒
航在時空中想你
除了冷冽
其實
你並非那麼——
遙不可及

That Winter 　　　　　　　　　　　　　　　Lin Ming-Li

Carefully
I open
One after another photo

Buried at the bottom of the trunk
Tinctured with the lapse of time
To exhibit the tidbits of time-honored stories

When the years
Move westward
The drunken spring is still asleep
The stone steps are rustling with withered leaves
Apricot flowers again take on new green
The wind, shuttles like butterflies while frolicking

And I
Anchor my thought in pause
In time-space to miss you
Except for chilliness
Actually
You are not —
Out of reach

✿ ✿ ✿

17 ·

同兒輩賦未開海棠二首（其一） 元好問

枝間新綠一重重，小蕾深藏數點紅。
愛惜芳心莫輕吐，且教桃李鬧春風。

Crabapple Flowers Before Blosssoming (No. 1)

Yuan Haowen

Green greening and bursting
layers upon layers among twigs

& branches; small buds, bits &
dots of red, are now concealing,

then revealing: they are hesitant
to blossom and heart-throb, in spite

of peaches & plums playfully
frolicking in the spring wind.

飛吧，我的蜂鳥   林明理

飛吧，我的蜂鳥
為了擁抱夢想
帶著堅強笑顏
穿著藍綠盛裝
飛向遠路盡處——
去找尋自己的巢

飛吧，我的蜂鳥
飛向雲彩或溪流
星星為妳鋪床
花兒簇擁入懷
就像個森林公主…
…通往星辰的征途

飛吧，我的蜂鳥
天空何其浩瀚
大地是妳的舞臺
為了擁抱夢想
在寂靜的遠方歌唱
也回到我的腦海

Keep Flying, My Hummingbird

　　　　　　　　　　　　Lin Ming-Li

Keep flying, my hummingbird
To embrace the fond dream
With an adamant smile
In glaringly blue and green costumes
To fly to the far end of the road —
In search of your own nest

Keep flying, my hummingbird
Towards the clouds or streams
The stars make bed for you
With an armful of flowers
Like a forest princess...
...The journey to the stars

Keep flying, my hummingbird
Big and boundless is the sky
The great earth is your stage
To embrace the fond dream
Singing in the silent distance
And echoing in my mind

🍃 🍃 🍃

18 ·

同兒輩賦未開海棠二首（其二）　　　元好問

翠葉輕籠豆顆勻，胭脂濃抹蠟痕新。
殷勤留著花梢露，滴下生紅可惜春。

元詩明理越千載
古今抒情詩三百首
漢英對照

Crabapple Flowers Before Blosssoming (No. 2)

Yuan Haowen

Gently enveloped with green
foliage, clusters of beans of crab-

apple blossoms, to which, seemingly,
wax-like rouge is heavily applied.

Filled with great affections, I want
to keep the dewdrops atop the flowery

twigs, lest they drop down through
the pitiable sight of crimson spring.

我的書房

林明理

深夜,書窗下
常亮著燈光
孤寂的鍵盤
伴隨我　默默書寫
遊歷的喜悅
對大自然的禮讚

我喜歡
坐看星辰起落
讓愛點綴人間淨土
在沉默中思悟
在寧靜中馳騁
一邊品茶
一邊醞釀著句——

林明理畫

我的書房

就像在無邊的海面
眺望一幅幅山水畫卷
　用心諦聽
世界便有了歌聲
　細細體味
心靈便浸潤了美好

My Study Lin Ming-Li

In deep night, under the window with a desk
It is constantly bright
The lonely keyboard
Accompanies me　to write in silence
The joy of travelling
Tribute to the great nature

I like
To watch while sitting the rising and falling of stars
　For love to dot and adorn the pure land of the world
Enlightenment in silence
Galloping in quiet
While sipping tea
Sentences structures are being brainstormed —

Just like the surface of a boundless sea
To gaze afar at one after another scroll of hills and rills
　　To listen carefully
And the world is aloud with songs
　　To savor with gusto
The heart is tinctured with kindness

19．

論詩三十首（其四）   元好問

一語天然萬古新，豪華落盡見真淳。
南窗白日羲皇上，未害淵明是晉人。

Poems on Poetry Composition (No. 4)
Yuan Haowen

Simple with natural words
& unaffected diction; shedding

all flowers, sincerity is seen
— this is the way of Tao

Yuanming, who styles himself
a homebody, or a person

of antiquity, yet he is a poet
of Jin dynasty, a trendsetter.

愛無疆域   林明理

對愛情有時同樂音般
一個音符輕起
宛若整個森林在旋轉
在沒有疆界之處
時間是唯一會呼吸的海洋

愛人啊，可曾將一切痛苦
一針一針地縫合？再穿上肺腑的冰雪，
即使切切的流泉

也是歌聲亂，顫顫索索
迎著低斜的紅太陽

誰說愛情是有希冀的方向？
是找不到真理的天堂？
是為愛而生的力量？
是絕對的孤獨，無法呼吸的想像？
如果可憫也算上相對的悲歡

愛情是宙斯沉默下急遽的心律聲
是一個夜夜聽到馬蹄
都會屏息以待的荒唐
是比星月還第一
游向遙遠無終的海岸

Love Is Boundless　　　　Lin Ming-Li

Sometimes love is like music
When a musical note is rising slowly
As if the whole forest is turning and whirling
Where there is no bound
Time is the only ocean that can breathe

Oh my love, do you seal all the pains
Stitch by stich? To put on the lungs of ice & snow,
Even the babbling water
Riotous of singing, shivering and trembling
Against the red sun slanting low

Who days love is the direction with a hope?
The paradise of truth is hard to find?

The strength born for love?
Absolute loneliness, imagination which cannot be breathed?
If pity can be counted as comparative joys and sorrows

Love is the quick rhythm of heart in the silent universe
The seaboard where the clip-clop of the horse is heard
From night to night, the absurdity of holding breath to wait
Earlier than the early moon and stars
Swimming afar to immensity

20 ·

論詩三十首（其十二）　　　　　　元好問

望帝春心托杜鵑，佳人錦瑟怨華年。
詩家總愛西昆好，獨恨無人作鄭箋。

Poems on Poetry Composition (No. 12)
Yuan Haowen

The overthrown emperor, sorrow-stricken,
dies to be reincarnated into a cuckoo-bird

who, with his blood-dripping beak, is twittering
plaintively in late spring. Each and every string

of the golden zither is reminiscent of the
vanished springs of a beauty. The poetry

of Li Shangyin is universally appreciated,
yet without annotators to its literary allusions.

傾聽紅松籽飄落   林明理

她在斜坡上漫步，宛如紅松籽飄落
雲氣冉冉的星空；
時間與天地稜線交錯
紡在她的紅髮和微笑間；
那阿波羅的杖，那琉璃瓦的雙眸
如此澄澈、如此恬靜，憂鬱卻靈動
在這片蔚然的長白山中
黑暗已輕挪著腳步下沉
傾聽紅松籽飄落
她細細思量
菖蒲的細語，羽翼的蟲鳴
在甜美的歌雀消逝後，
全都鏽蝕而閒置，一剎那
稀微的碎影　覆蓋山丘。

Listen to Red Pine Seeds Dropping Down
                                    Lin Ming-Li

She is strolling on the slope, like red pine seeds dropping down
The starry cloudy sky;
Time and heaven & earth intertwine with each other
Amidst her red hair and beaming smiles;
The cane of Apollo, the eyes of glazed tiles
So limpid, so sedate, so melancholy and animated
In the boundless Changpai Mountain
Darkness is move steps downward
Listen to red pine seeds dropping down
She carefully ponders

The whisper of flag leaves, chirping of winged insects
After the sweet songbirds disappear,
All are rusty to be idle, in an instant
The dim shattered shadows   to cover up hills and mounds.

21·

論詩三十首（其十九） 元好問

萬古幽人在澗阿，百年孤憤竟如何？
無人說與天隨子，春草輸贏較幾多？

Poems on Poetry Composition (No. 19)
Yuan Haowen

The recluse-poet resides in
a riverside abode — what about

one hundred years of noble
rage? Nobody to share it with

Lu Guimeng, a famous poet of
Tang dynasty, who abandons

himself to the game of competition
in the strength of grass blades for fun.

因為愛 林明理

因為愛
那真切之吻

已戰勝卑怯的恐懼。
在妳的無瑕
和時間的
繪影中
它彷若一滴雨露；

看著妳
靈巧而專注，
只想把自己的
思想水手給妳。
當溫暖的山谷裡
不再佈滿荊棘之際
看命運如何聯繫我們
極其相像的故事。

Owing to Love　　　　　　　　Lin Ming-Li

Owing to love
The genuine kiss
Has subdued the cowardly horror.
In your business
And the picture
Of time
It is like a drop of rain;

Looking at you
Flexible and attentive,
Intending to give his
thought-sailor to you.
When the warm valley is no
longer choked with thorns
see how fate connects us
very similar stories.

元詩明理揉千載
古今抒情詩三百首
漢英對照

22 ·

論詩三十首（其二十二）　　　　　　元好問

奇外無奇更出奇，一波才動萬波隨。
只知詩到蘇黃盡，滄海橫流卻是誰？

Poems on Poetry Composition (No. 22)　　　Yuan Haowen

Beyond wonders there are wonders
which are more wonderful; a wave is

waving upon another undulating wave:
myriads of waving waves. Poetry seems

to have exhausted itself upon Su Shi
and Huang Tingjian, two famous poets

in Song dynasty; but who — who are
making further waves upon waves?

黑夜無法將你的光和美拭去　　　　　　林明理

當地平線第一道黎明
向沉睡中的你歌唱
牧場在潺潺小溪的霧雲下甦醒
所有的眼睛都注視著
你，活著的意志，眉宇的神情

已不再遲鈍沉悶
你像遠空之鷹
在翠嶺間自由穿行
聽萬木的呼吸，雛鳥的輕啼
那蜜蜂，正採擷清甜的汁液

縱然剎那，就讓宙斯尋思
為你而閃明，在綠蔭的沉默裡
旋律從我心底響起，在你遠離之際
黑夜無法將你的光和美拭去
　　　　噢，如果眾人之主聽得見
我真切地祝禱，而地域也不再有距離
就讓這峽谷捲起回音吧
細弱的和風已頻頻翹首
在這條石徑上緩行
萬木跟著你的腳步而揮手
你篇章的詩情
確已創造了人間的泉源，萬古常青

The Dark Night Fails to Wipe Out Your Beauty and Light　　Lin Ming-Li

When the first dawning light in the horizon
Sings to you who are sound asleep
The pasture wakes up under the clouds over the babbling creek
All the eyes are attentive
On you, the living will, the expression in the eyes
No more drowsy and sluggish
You are like an eagle in the boundless sky
Freely flying among emerald mountains

Listen to the breath of myriads of trees, the gentle chirping of young birds
The bees are gathering sweet juice

In an instant, for Zeus to meditate
To flash for you, in the silence of the green shade
The melody is arising from the bottom of my heart, upon your leaving afar
The dark night fails to wipe out your beauty and light
           Oh, if the leader of the crowd can hear it
Honestly I pray, and there is no distance between regions
Let the valley be aloud with echoes
The gentle breeze is on the stirring
Slowly creeping along the stony path
Myriads of trees follow your steps while waving hands
The poetry of your pieces
Has really created a fountain in the world, forever green

23 ·

論詩三十首（其二十四）   元好問

有情芍藥含春淚，無力薔薇臥晚枝。
拈出退之山石句，始知渠是女郎詩。

Poems on Poetry Composition (No. 24)
       Yuan Haowen

Peony flowers, sentimental,
are watery with teardrops;

sickly roses, bathed in morning
twilight, are spreading and

sprawling. — such lines
by Qin Guan are feeble and

feminine before the virile and
masculine style of Han Yu.

行經河深處 林明理

行經河深處
我心思索
一簇簇柳叢滴瀝著孤寂
野兔開溜在懸崖絕壁
一隻夜鴉在谷中
對著煙霧彌漫的月影搖顫
在這裡 我繫不羈之心於河船
而你仍在不可知的他鄉

何曾為我守候
訴說那樸素壯麗的靈魂有多麼激昂：
天地間更沒有一顆明星
把你最深的痛苦告訴我
是怎樣的夢輕盈地落在我燃燒的心上
讓我們的愛情長成金黃的麥海
那失去驕傲，失去所有的
我，用困倦的目光，還朝著麥海繼續飛翔

Through Depth of the River Lin Ming-Li

Through depth of the river
My heart is pondering

Clusters of willow are dripping with loneliness
Wild rabbits are running on steep precipices and cliffs
A nightingale in the valley
Shaking against the moon suffusing with mist
Here I tether my free heart to the riverside boat
You are still in an unknown land

When to guard for me
To tell how impassioned the simple and sublime soul is:
Between heaven and earth there is not a single star
To tell me your deepest sorrow
What kind of dream to gently alight on my burning heart
Let our love grow into the golden sea of wheat
Deprived of pride and all
I, with my weary eyes, continue my flight in the direction of the sea of wheat

24 ·

杏花雜詩三首（其一） 元好問

杏花牆外一枝橫，半面宮妝出曉晴。
看盡春風不回首，寶兒元自太憨生。

Three Poems on Apricot Flowers (No. 1)
Yuan Haowen

Blatant is a twig of apricot
flowers without the wall, like

a palace maid protruding herself
to see the outside world. Bathed

and intoxicated in the spring wind,
the Cute Baby, concubine of Emperor

Yang of Sui, is enjoying the spring
wind without turning her head.

愛無畏懼 　　　　　　　　　　　　　　林明理

愛，無需冠冕堂皇的
道理
或虛偽的正義
我清楚地知道
當我離世
我會記得
那些我曾開車兜風
經過的大海　溪流
或雲朵的微笑
我會記得

生命的脆弱與堅強
走過的高低起伏
以及真正的渴望
來自心靈的平靜
和樂　　就能溫暖
至於愛
只要順著平行的維度
沒有猶豫，因為
猶豫容易敗北
愛是光亮，是一切

Love Without Fear

Lin Ming-Li

No need for love to be fancy
With a reason
Or false justice
I know clearly that
When I die
I still remember
The days when I drive for fun
Passing streams & seas
Or the breaming smiles of clouds
I will remember

The fragility and strength of life
The ups and downs
Ambitions in a real sense
Tranquility of mind
And joys can bring warmth
As for love
So long as the parallel dimensions are followed
Without hesitations, because
Hesitations lead to failure
Love is light, and everything

25.

杏花雜詩三首（其二）

元好問

嫋嫋纖條映酒船，綠嬌紅小不勝憐。
長年自笑情緣在，猶要春風慰眼前。

Three Poems on Apricot Flowers (No. 2)

Yuan Haowen

A wine boat is caressed by
willow twigs which are lean

and lank; tender green and
small red constitute a loveable

scene. Constant laughing in
spite of myself: with the fullness

of my heart, spring wind is
an indispensable comforter.

紅櫻樹下
　　　　　　　　　　　　　　　　　　林明理

葉縫之光
在冰枝的榆蔭裏
瀉進

一道白煙
將四圍圈將起來
從兩重山腰串過
隱隱的
除隆隆的輪聲
之外
落花如疏雨似的
貼著人身
而你的眼睛卻
明得似火

一瞬間
風也開始結巴地
說不出話

Under Sakura Trees   Lin Ming-Li

Light through the leaves
In the shade of the icy twigs
Pouring into

A beam of white mist
Encircled and enveloped
Through two mountainsides
Dimly
Except for the rumbling
Wheels
Falling flowers like a sparse rainfall
Close to human body
And your eyes
Bright like fire

In an instant
The wind begins to stutter
Deprived of words

🌿 🌿 🌿

26·

杏花雜詩八首（其五）   元好問

紛紛紅紫不勝稠，爭得春光競出頭。
卻是梨花高一著，隨宜梳洗盡風流。

Eight Poems on Apricot Flowers (No. 5)

Yuan Haowen

Heavy clusters of red &
purple, apricot flowers

are striving for spring to
have one's day and to have

one's way, when pear blossoms
are detached: it remains itself,

never to fail and fade in spite of
lashing winds & beating rains.

思念似雪花緘默地飛翔

林明理

思念似雪花緘默地飛翔
從地球彼端
沿著一條直線
穿越長長的山巒和河水
來回走動
引我期盼
就這樣把它迎進了門窗

我是顆渺小的水滴
自我耽溺於
一片廣闊的天空
當我緩緩地搖晃
落在大雪漫天的夜晚
啊,我想要歡呼
有什麼比得上你強大的靈魂
和那神采奕奕的光芒

元詩明理楚千載
古今抒情詩三百首
漢英對照

Thoughts Fly Silently Like Snowflakes
Lin Ming-Li

Thoughts fly silently like snowflakes
From the other side of the earth
Along a straight line
Through long and meandering rivers and mountains
Back and forth
Soliciting my expectation
To welcome them into my door and window

I am a tiny drop of water
Self-indulged
In a boundless sky
When I slowly shake and shiver
Into the night veiled with heavy snow
Ah, I want to cheer and acclaim
What is comparable to your powerful soul
And your radiant light

🌳 🌳 🌳

27 ·

遊天壇雜詩
元好問

湍聲洶洶落懸崖，見說蛟龍擘石開。
安得天瓢一翻倒，躡雲平下看風雷。

A Poem on the Heaven Temple Mountain
Yuan Haowen

Great noises from the falling waterfall against the cliff; it is said a huge

dragon has cleft open the huge rock,
hence the waterfall. How to over-

turn the heavenly ladle and add
water to the waterfall, to watch,

through the clouds, the spectacle
of water swelling into a tempest?

在那山海之間　　　　　　　　　　　　林明理

在古城和沉思的海岸間，
我小小的夢漫遊著。我喜愛——
遨遊西西里島遠甚其他之地，
所以沿它的老路走，我將
憩止於內布羅迪山脈之一隅，
猶如乘著一彎彩虹，橫跨時空，
我想唱給妳聽，噢，美麗的倫札，
——雲和天，第勒尼安海。
在那山海之間，
妳，恰似一條聖光的溪流。

Between the Mountains and the Sea
                                    Lin Ming-Li

Between the ancient city and the pensive coast,
My little dream is roaming. I like travelling
To the Sicily far better than other places
Therefore, along its old road, I will
Rest and stop at a corner of the Nebrodi Mountains
As if riding a rainbow, striding time-space,
I want to sing for you, oh, beautiful Lenza,

元詩明理達千載
古今抒情詩三百首
漢英對照

— Clouds and sky, Tyrrhenian Sea.
Between the mountains and the sea,
You, like a stream of holy light.

❦ ❦ ❦

28 ·

京都元夕　　　　　　　　　　元好問

袨服華妝著處逢，六街燈火鬧兒童。
長衫我亦何為者，也在遊人笑語中。

The Lantern Festival in the Capital
Yuan Haowen

Splendid attire and gaudy
clothes everywhere; large

streets and small lanes are
bright with festive lanterns,

children frolicking. As a
long gown wearer, I am

engulfed in happy laughters
and cheerful voices.

秋日的港灣　　　　　　　　　　林明理

流動的時光羅織著晚浪
與幽微的漁火。

一片無人注意的蚵棚，
在鹹澀的雨中。

蘆花回蕩的挽歌
被秋風輕輕挾起，移步向前。
古堡則把我的眼波下錨
繫住所有的懷念。

The Harbor in Autumn　　　　　Lin Ming-Li

The moving time is netting the evening tide
And the dim fishing light.
A stretch of ignored shed of oyster,
Soaked in the salty rain.

The elegies reverberating through the reeds
Gently lifted up by the autumn wind, moving forward.
The old castle anchorages my eyes
To hold all my yearnings and memories.

🌳 🌳 🌳

29・

梁園春五首（其一）　　　　　元好問

軍從南去三回勝，雪自冬來二尺強。
今歲長春多樂事，內家應舉萬年觴。

元詩明理撼千載
古今抒情詩三百首
漢英對照

Five Poems on a Gardenful of Spring (No. 1)
Yuan Haowen

Military expeditions from the south
with several victories; there is, since

the beginning of winter, almost a
meter-high accumulation of snow. This

spring is a long spring filled with a great
number of joys and happy events, for

which the palace shall be festive with
great celebrations for long-lasting blessing.

亭溪行　　　　　　　　　　　　林明理

晴巒樹石雲浮空，悠緩炊煙連山濛。
四面晚風掩村舍，回眸亭溪已成翁。

Strolling Along the Pavilion Creek
Lin Ming-Li

Hills and stones and trees bathed
in the sunshine, clouds floating

in the sky; the leisurely kitchen
smoke is dim and distant from

mountain to mountain. The evening
wind all about is blowing over

the cottages; a backward glance at
the pavilion creek, an old man now.

🌱🌱🌱

30 ·

山居雜詩（其一） 元好問

瘦竹藤斜掛，幽花草亂生。
林高風有態，苔滑水無聲。

Miscellaneous Poems About the Mountain Life (No. 1)
Yuan Haowen

Lean bamboos and
vines flying aslant;

secluded flowers and
wild, tumbled grass.

A tall forest takes the
shape of the wind; over

slippery moss, the water
is running noiselessly.

嵩山之夢[9] 林明理

高高地
在如此多的山之間
我迷失了
如一隻歌雀奔向叢林

---

[9] 嵩山位於河南省，是五嶽的中嶽。

元詩明理達千載
古今抒情詩三百首
漢英對照

銜著綠色的夢
當七彩的靈光　耀滿山頭

啊，我飛翔
當沉睡的地殼呼喚我
真的嗎
這是夯土築城的亳都
真的嗎
這是站成永恆的佛寺

這奇異的峻峰
是夢，又不是夢
我迷失了
連秋月與星空
嵩陽書院
也溶進了我遐想的心

啊，我飛翔
北瞰黃河和洛水
南覽潁水和箕山
面對林立宮觀
我合十
是的，我還要跟山水對話

飛過博物院和觀星台
飛過古城、關隘和戰場
穿過白雲和山風
心　卻一直醒著
聽戲曲聲聲
一顆心　也被鎖住了

啊，我飛翔
在茶樓
在巷弄
我翹首向來路張望
那些早已過去
如煙的往事已化為微笑

深深地
聽見了海峽的呼吸
感到了月亮的孤獨
我匆匆地來
卻迷失了
迷失在讚美嵩山的那一瞬

The Dream of Songshan Mountain[10]

Lin Ming-Li

High and lofty
Among so many mountains
I am lost
Like a vocal sparrow flying to the woods
Holding in its beak a green dream
When the light of seven colors   is glaring atop the mountains

Oh, I fly
When the slumbering earth is calling me
Really?
This is the capital constructed with rammed earth
Really?
This is the Buddhist temple standing into eternity

---

[10] The Songshan Mountain is located in Henan Province, the middle mountain of the five mountains.

The eerie peaks
A dream, and not a dream
I am lost
Together with autumn moon and the starry sky
Songyang Academy
Also merging into my heart of fantasy

Oh, I fly
Northward look at the Yellow River and the Luoshui River
Southward look at the Yingshui River and the Jishan Mountain
Facing the forest of palaces
I cross my fingers
Yes, I'll have a dialogue with hills and rills

Flying into the museum and the Star Observation Platform
Flying over the ancient town, mountain pass and battleground
Through white clouds and mountain wind
The heart   remains awake
Aloud is the traditional Chinese opera
A heart is also locked up

Oh, I fly
In the teahouse
In the lanes
I crane my neck in the direction of the way here
Those smiles have been past
The mist-like past events have turned into beaming smiles

Profoundly
I hear the breath of the Straits
I feel the loneliness of the moon
I come in a hurry
But am lost
In the instant in praise of the Songshan Mountain

元朝 Yuan Dynasty

31.

題龍陽縣青草湖　　　　　　　　唐珙

西風吹老洞庭波，一夜湘君白髮多。
醉後不知天在水，滿船清夢壓星河。

To the Green Grass Lake　　　　Tang Gong

Waters in Dongting Lake
have been blown old by

autumn wind; the Water
Goddess is white-crowned

overnight. Drunken, I know
not the Milky Way is in

water: a boatful of clear
dreams upon the starry river.

秋暮　　　　　　　　　　　　林明理

冬山河　鹹草鳴蛩
濱鷸　兩兩
惟有小水鴨
擾亂了整個水面
喚起白霧飛脫

元詩明理搓千載
古今抒情詩三百首
漢英對照

留下溪口外
一片明霞

Autumn Dusk   Lin Ming-Li

Dongshan River   insects chirping through salty grass
The dunlin   in pairs
Only ducklings
Have disturbed the water surface
Hence a flight of white fog
And beyond the creek mouth
A patch of twilight glow

✤ ✤ ✤

32 ·

觀梅有感   劉因

東風吹落戰塵沙，夢想西湖處士家。
只恐江南春意減，此心原不為梅花。

Inspired by Plum Blossoms   Liu Yin

Spring wind blows off dust filmed
on the plum trees, when I am

dreaming about the recluse as
a plum grower by the West Lake.

Worry: the spring in the Southern
Shore might be weakened and

shortened, instead of plum blossoms,
which are blossoming glaringly.

我瞧見⋯   林明理

1.
在這海濱草地上,一群潛鳥
唱著我似懂非懂的歌,
即使風在訕笑——我們仍成了知己。

2.
總有一天我會
在你必經的老雲杉上,用野百合的
春歌,同你聊聊天。

3.
我願是紅腹濱鷸,
飛越千里⋯
只為了相聚時分秒不差。

I Saw⋯   Lin Ming-Li

1.
On the coastal meadow, a flock of loons
Are singing songs which I half understand,
Even if the wind is laughing — we have become close friends.

2.
Some day I will
On the old spruce trees which you daily pass by, with the spring song
Of wild lilies, to chat with you.

3.
I wish I were a red knot,
Flying through thousands of miles…
Just to get together at the sharp time.

33·

師師檀板　　　　　　　　　　　　　瞿佑

千金一曲擅歌場，曾把新腔動帝王。
老大可憐人事改，縷衣檀板過湖湘。

Li Shishi, a Famous Courtezan-Musician　　Qu You

A piece of music is worth much
more than much, the charming

singing of Li Shishi, a famous
courtezan-musician, has ever

charmed the emperor. The lapse
of time spells the lapse of her youth,

when she makes a simple living
by singing as a common singer.

影子　灑落愛丁堡上　　　　　　　林明理

這是一幅水墨畫
濃淡層次

被你繪描
薄暮中，誰的
影子在長嘆？
半幅未完　老城倨傲
老的不是古堡
是我髮稍

The Shadow Is Splashed on Edinburgh
　　　　　　　　　　　　　　　　Lin Ming-Li

This is a wash painting
In pale shades
Painted by you
In twilight, whose
Shadow is sighing a long sigh?
The half-finished painting　the old city is proud
What is old is not the ancient castle
But the end of my hair

34 •

過湖口望廬山　　　　　　　　　方回

江行初見雪中梅，梅雨霏微棹始回。
莫道無人肯相送，廬山猶自過江來。

Viewing the Lushan Mountain After Crossing the Lake
　　　　　　　　　　　　　　　Fang Hui

Boating on the river, initial sight
of plum blossoms in snow, which

are drizzling like rain, showers after
showers — before the turning of the

boat. Say not that nobody comes to
see me off — the Lushan Mountain,

whose silhouette is exhibiting
itself, crosses the river by itself.

愛的實現 　　　　　　　　　　　　林明理

我站在帷幕的光影下
面對觀眾的一片驚愕
以歌,以風中之舞,以飛鳥的孤單嚮慕
輕柔地用腳尖跳開。演出自己像一湖水
漾著溶溶的月,只有在被舟子蕩槳
的黑影浮動中才可聽到嘆息的蘆葉

對岸那棵白楊等了三千個夜才把身影拉長
綠柳,荷花、海燕
全都冒雨迎風趕來西堤赴會而又消逝為
一片星光,或許你已忘記十年不變的諾言
諾言,其實無法實現
偶然回首,今年的蘆葦又雪白了頭

The Fulfilment of Love 　　　　　Lin Ming-Li

I stand under the curtain of light & shadow
To face the audience's amazement
With a song, with a dance in the wind, with the lonely bird
To gently jump away with the toes. Self-performing like a
lakeful of water

Rippling with a dissolved moon, only in the dark shadow
Of the floating boat can the sigh of the reed leaves be heard

The opposite-bank aspen tree has waited for three thousand nights to stretch the figure
Green willows, lotus flowers, sea swallows
All come to the West Bank braving the wind & rain to taper off
Into a beam of starlight, perhaps you have forgotten the ten years of promise
Actually, a promise cannot be fulfilled
Occasional looking back, the reed of this year is again white-crowned

🌳 🌳 🌳

35 •

客舍雨   熊禾

青煙著雨傍樓橫，輾轉虛窗夢不成。
客裡清愁無可奈，臥聽簷溜瀉秋聲。

The Hotel Rain   Xiong He

Mist in the rain is rampant over
the towers & mansions; tossing

and turning, unable to sleep against
the empty window. A wanderer

is helpless about the pure sorrow,
through which the straggler is giving

ear to raindrops from the eaves —
a cascade of autumnal whispers.

思念似穿過月光的鯨群之歌   林明理

思念似穿過月光的鯨群之歌
緩慢而綿長⋯

我傾聽，有時它驟然而降
每一個音符都清晰純淨
無法移動──

而那些沉溺其中的記憶
如我在讀你的時光

Yearning Is Like the Song of a School of Whales Through the Moonlight

Lin Ming-Li

Yearning is like the song of a school of whales through the moonlight
Slow and lingering⋯

I listen, and it drops all of a sudden
Each musical note is clear and pure
Immovable —

And those memories steeped in it
Like me who is reading your time

36・

題李鶴田穆陵大事記後 　　　　　　劉詵

陵寢巍峨十二闌，西興吹角浙江寒。
老臣無限遺弓淚，寫與人間異代看。

The Afterword 　　　　　　Liu Shen

Twelve imperial tombs which
tower majestically; horn

blowing at the ferry of Xixing,
and Zhejiang is cold. The old

minister bosoms boundless regrets
with tears welling up in his eyes,

which is written down for readers
through the future generations.

崖邊的流雲 　　　　　　林明理

我飛涉了千年　盼過無數個冬
忽而想起了妳
在左岸的水面
凝諦野玫瑰似的雪
或者是尋找這夜的紅黑
那碧湖的眼睛
把時空遮攔起來
連白樺林都掩蓋了

直到岩壁上都留下風的見證
於是我再一次
飛涉千年
是追回細膩的道別
或者是焚燒這夜的紅黑
那碧湖的眼睛
眼睛也和陽光一樣忠實
在每絲雪裡都拂拭著一聲歎息

Flowing Clouds Over the Cliff

Lin Ming-Li

I have been flying for thousands of years　yearning for countless winters
Suddenly I remember you
Over the water of the left bank
Attentively listen to the snow which is like wild roses
Or in search of the red and black of the night
The eyes of the blue lake
Block the time and space
Even the woods of white birch are screened

Until the rocky wall is with the trace of the wind
And once more I
Fly through thousands of years
Is this the recalling of the farewell
Or the red and black of the night burning
That eyes with the blue of the lake
The eyes are as loyal as the sunshine
To wipe off each sigh from each slice o

✤ ✤ ✤

37.

題陳渭叟紫雲編　　　　　　　　葉森

一度詩來一見君，只應芳杜襲蘭薰。
有時寫到遊仙句，繞筆秋香生紫雲。

An Inscription　　　　　　　　Ye Sen

Composing a poem, I
come to see you; among

a mass of flowers orchid
flowers are being fragrant.

Occasionally a wandering
line of poetry is inspired,

the writing brush is moist
& misty with purple clouds.

秋夕　　　　　　　　　　　　林明理

無關四季流轉，在身處的後山
我都深信不疑：
我會盡量想起你的話語
微笑和帶有憂鬱的氣息

讓那川流不止的思念
變成一道流星雨，
投射到我牆垛之前
我將說出自己秘密藏在哪裡

The Autumn Eve Lin Ming-Li

Irrelevant to the turning of seasons, in the mountain behind me
I firmly believe:
I will try to remember your words
Beaming and the melancholy breath

For the yearning which runs nonstop
To become a meteor shower,
To be projected before my wall
I will tell the hiding place of my secret

🌳 🌳 🌳

38 ·

隱居松 張雨

露壇棲妙蔭，仙籟降靈芬。
何時三易帔，重拂兩梢雲。

The Hermit-Pine-Tree Zhang Yu

The open-air platform
is patterned with a wonder-

ful shade; fairy grass is
shivering with ethereal

music. When the silk shawl
is changed for three times,

two masses of clouds are
whisked and re-whisked.

冀望   林明理

1.
我在黑暗中，
看見了光⋯
但並不是非比尋常。

2.
我沒有任何智語可說，
因為，上主，
是我堅持下去的理由。

Hope   Lin Ming-Li

1.
In darkness
I see the light…
But not so extraordinary.

2.
I have no wise words to say,
Because, God,
Is the reason for me to carry on.

39 ·

絕句 趙孟頫

春寒惻惻掩重門,金鴨香殘火尚溫。
燕子不來花又落,一庭風雨自黃昏。

A Quatrain Zhao Mengfu

Sad and sentimental, a cold
spring sees a closed door after

another closed door; the duck-
shaped stove is still warm with

a hangover fire. Before the coming
of swallows, flowers begin to fade

and fall, when a yardful of winds
& rains constitute a solitary dusk.

讓愛自由 林明理

我不相信,
愛,必須先學會妥協,
惟有讓它像蒼鷹,──
向夢想飛馳,
既不存畏懼,
也絕不忘卻自由。
在愛的純淨的光波裡,
每個清晨,
都帶來誠摯的一天。
只要虔信愛情,

我將終生為它努力。
因為愛,
是我一生中最難忘的章節。

Let Love Be Free   Lin Ming-Li

I do not believe,
In love, one must learn to compromise.
Only let it be like an eagle —
Flying in the direction of the dream,
Without fear,
Yet not to forget freedom.
In the pure light of love,
Each morning,
Brings a sincere day.
With faith in love,
I'll work for it all my life.
Because love
Is the most unforgettable chapter in my life.

絕句   釋英

正月梅花落,二月桃花紅。
榮枯元有數,不必怨東風。

A Quatrain   Shi Ying

The second moon sees
plum blossoms fading and

falling; the third moon is
fair with red peach flowers.

Blossoming & withering, birth
& death, all is doomed by fate

— the blame shall not be
shifted onto the spring wind.

二〇〇九年冬天　　　　　　　　　　　　林明理

蕭蕭黃桐葉，像挽歌的茶花女
在屋檐那兩盞沉默的
燈火間，一首老歌兀自唱起
流光的記憶
飛向濕漉漉的十字街頭

像胡同裡誦經的木魚
緊咒的落雪
正張著清澈的眼眸，任意念羅織成
一張攢在心底的輪廓
怎忍冬風
把露宿的疏葉一一吹走？

The Winter of 2009　　　　　　　Lin Ming-Li

Yellow phoenix tree leaves are rustling, the lady of camellias
like a dirge
Under the eaves two silent
Lamps, an old song is being sung suddenly
The memory of flowing time
Flying to the moist crisscross streets

Like a wooden fish chanting sutras in an alley
The tight spell of falling snow
With clear eyes open, for ideas to be woven
Into a profile stowed away in the heart
Unbearable: for the winter wind
To blow away one after another sparse leaf sleeping in the open?

41 ·

上京即事 薩都剌

紫塞風高弓力強，王孫走馬獵沙場。
呼鷹腰箭歸來晚，馬上倒懸雙白狼。

A Hunting Scene — Sa Dula

High wind beyond the Great
Wall, strong bows; princes &

young men are riding on flying
horses across the hunting ground.

Calling hawks with arrows on
their waists, they go home against

the setting sun, the horse laden
with a pair of hunted wolves.

帕德嫩神廟[11]

林明理

坐在巨石柱旁的大樹下
想像老城是怎樣變成今日的樣子
　　怎樣貫穿時間的秘辛
我向巨大穹蒼仰視
河水依舊不斷奔流
　　密談著愛琴海的神話故事

Dr. Mingli Lin painting work in Taiwan／The Patrhenon
帕德嫩神廟／林明理畫作

The Patrhenon[12]

Lin Ming-Li

Sitting under a big tree by the giant marble column
I imagine how the old city has become what it is today
What is its secret of passing through time
I look up at the boundless sky
The river keeps running forward
Chatting about the myth of the Aegean Sea

---

[11] 奉祀雅典娜女神的帕德嫩神廟（The Patrhenon）是古希臘文明的重要史蹟之一，這座擁有二千五百多年歷史的城市廢墟，座落在雅典衛城（Acropolis）之巔，俯瞰著希臘首都雅典（Athens）。

[12] The Parthenon, in memory of Athena, is one of the important historical relics of ancient Greece. Boasting a history of 2,500 years, the ruins of the city is situated atop the Athenian Acropolis, overlooking Athens, the capital of Greece.

🌳 🌳 🌳

42 •

過高郵射陽湖 　　　　　　　　　薩都刺

飄蕭樹梢風，淅瀝湖上雨。
不見打魚人，菰浦雁相語。

Passing by the Sheyang Lake 　　Sa Dula

The treetop is rustling and
whistling with spells of

wind; the lake is noisy with
a shower after another shower

of rain. Not a fisherman, not
an angler in sight, except for

the geese honking in mush-
room-shaped masses of reed.

寫給科爾多瓦[13]猶太教堂的歌 　　林明理

當我走向你，科爾多瓦，
走向古城，走向百花巷，

---

[13] 科爾多瓦（Córdoba）位於西班牙安達盧西亞自治區、瓜達爾基維爾河畔，是哥多華省的首府，也是一個擁有許多文化遺產和古蹟的城市。其中的猶太教堂，古老而莊嚴，牆上雕飾著希伯來文是出自猶太人的巧匠邁蒙尼德（Maimonides）。在猶太教堂內有座他的半身雕塑，在附近的百花巷中也有一座他的全身雕塑，他也是著名的猶太哲學家、法學家和醫生。

走向靜寂的猶太教堂，
走向聖潔的九燭台，
走向風中的荒涼聲響，
走向邁蒙尼德的雕像，
這時，你的沉默如葉飄落，
是我眸中晶瑩的水花。

啊，神啊，我的全能，
祢的慈悲光耀世道，
祢的福音在黑暗中浮現。
請支撐祢的子民，
撫平歷史的傷痕。
在這和平的早晨，
聽我無聲的祈禱。
阿門。

A Song for the Cordoba[14] Synagogue

Lin Ming-Li

When I walk toward you, Cordoba,
Toward the city, toward the Flowery Lane,
Toward the silent synagogue,
Toward the holy nine candlesticks,
Toward the desolate sound in the wind,

---

[14] Cordoba is in the Spanish autonomous region of Andalusia, the Guadalquivir River, and it is the capital of Cordoba province, with rich cultural heritage and a host of historical sites. The synagogue, ancient and stately, has its walls decorated with Hebrew by the hand of Maimonides, a Jewish craftsman. In the synagogue, there is a bust sculpture of him, and in the neighborhood Flowery Lane there is a full sculpture of his body. He is also a famous Jewish philosopher, jurist and physician.

Near the statue of Maimonides,
Your silence drops like falling leaves,
To become the crystal sprays in my eyes.

Ah, deity, my Almighty,
Your mercy shines on the mortal world,
Your gospel emerges from darkness.
Please support your people,
While healing the historical wounds.
In this peaceful morning,
Listen to my silent prayer.
Amen.

43 ·

秋夜聞笛　　　　　　　　　　　　薩都刺

何人吹笛秋風外？北固山前月色寒。
亦有江南未歸客，徘徊終夜倚闌幹。

Fluting in an Autumn Night　　　Sa Dula

Who is fluting beyond the autumn
wind? Beigu Hill is distinct in

the moonlight, when the chilly
beams engender a universal sense

of cold. Some wanderer, delayed
in the southern land, is strolling

aimlessly against the balustrade —
throughout a night after another night.

笛在深山中 林明理

風吹飄然，誰家
笛聲在迴盪，迴盪
這清寒的深山
我拉開蒼穹
那守在雲間的白頂如金銀般閃爍

雨，輕輕地凝住
凝住，又溜進
葉心的層樓
披起煙光
被群山佇候，卻消逝於暮色

沿湖走過
笛聲遠，留長空
當春雪飛落竹屋
映照我心底的月影
是否也上升凝託行雲？

Fluting in the Deep Mountain Lin Ming-Li

Wind blowing, which home
Is aloud with fluting, and echoing
In the cool deep mountain
I draw open the vault
The white top in the clouds glitters like gold and silver

Rain, gently freezes
Freezes, before gliding in again

The layers of tower of the leaves
Wrapping in smoke and light
Waited upon by the mountains, to disappear in the dusk

Walking about the lake
The fluting is from afar, in the boundless space
When spring snow flies and falls onto the bamboo hut
To shine upon the moon shadow in the bottom of my heart
Does it fly with the wafting clouds?

44 •

池荷　　　　　　　　　　　　　　黃庚

紅藕花多映碧欄，秋風才起易凋殘。
池塘一段榮枯事，都被沙鷗冷眼看。

Pond Lotus Blossoms　　　　Huang Geng

Masses of red lotus blossoms
against the green balustrade;

initial movement of the autumn
wind, and there is withering.

An episode of thriving
and wilting, in such a small

pond, is witnessed by the gull
with a detached, cold eye.

清雨塘   林明理

野花飛落,雨繞樹輕舞
池面,像綠蔭的春野
在纏路的水草底下
映出永不退縮的天邊

遊魚笑語低昂
月意是久別重逢的杳然
夜啊,一片雪花消融的哀音
讓天地互相傳看

The Pond of Limpid Rain   Lin Ming-Li

Wild flowers fading and flying, raindrops drop gently about the tree
The pond surface, like the spring field in green shade
Under the water plants which are tangled on the way
To mirror the sky which never recedes

The swimming fish are gurgling
The sense of the moon is meeting after a long separation
Oh, night, the sad sound of a flake of snow melting
For the heaven and earth to see each other

江村即事   黃庚

江村暝色漸淒迷。數點殘鴉雜雁飛。
雁宿蘆花鴉宿樹,各分一半夕陽歸。

A Riverside Village 　　　　　Huang Geng

A riverside village, it is
darkening, to be misty and

murky; a few dots of remnant
ducks are flying amidst bevies

of wild geese. The wild geese
lodge for the night in the reeds,

and the ducks, in the trees; each
with a half sun, setting, and sinking.

山間小路　　　　　　　　　　林明理

深入山丘的陰影
細細領略
臘梅的清香

遠樹凝寂
從寺塔鐘樓走出
在墨潑間
在花雨上

想心定的水塘
被日落的叢林圍繞
從許多蜿蜒的小路
遠離霧氣的瀰漫在村莊

A Path in the Mountain 　　Lin Ming-Li

Into the shadow of mountain
To sense carefully
The faint scent of wintersweet

Still are the remote trees
Out of the bell tower of the temple
The instant of ink spreading
On the flowery rain

The pool is ready to calm down
And is surrounded by the woods caught in the setting sun
From a lot of meandering paths
Away from the village veiled in mist

46 ·

暮景   黃庚

浮雲開合晚風輕，白鳥飛邊落照明。
一曲彩虹橫界斷，南山雷雨北山晴。

A Dusk Scene   Huang Geng

Floating clouds open to close,
the evening breeze light; white

birds flit and fly through the
setting sun which is still bright.

A colorful rainbow cuts across
the scene: the southern hill is

caught in a thunderstorm and
the northern hill: fair and clear.

在匆匆一瞥間　　　　　　　　　　　林明理

黃昏的海鳥拍動著寒意…
我們的腳步聲
恍若越過潮汐和許多山峰,
從紅牆的迴廊樹蔭,
到落日瞇著銀藍的眼瞳。

我好想停在山的高處,
像馬兒豎起耳朵——
聽聽朝向彼端海岸的天空,
然後一派輕鬆地…
…親近了你,這就是我。

A Fleeting Glimpse　　　　　　　Lin Ming-Li

The seabirds at dusk are fluttering with a chill ...
The sound of our footfalls
Seemingly rises over the tides and a host of peaks,
From the tree shadows in the red-walled cloister,
To the setting sun that is squinting its silver-blue eye.

How I want to stay on the height of the mountain,
Like a horse pricking up its ears —
Listen to the sky stretching toward the coast beyond,
Then with great ease…
…Walk close to you, and this is me.

元詩明理接千載
古今抒情詩三百首
漢英對照

47·

江鄉夜興　　　　　　　　　　　尹延高

極浦霜清雁打圍,漁燈明滅水煙微。
天寒想是鱸魚少,犬吠空汀船夜歸。

Night of the Riverside Village　Yin Yengao

The remote water is clear with
frost where wild geese are frolicking;

fishing lamps flicker and flutter
through dim mist over the water.

A cold day sees fewer swimming
perches, when dogs are barking

through the empty river which
carries the boat homeward.

午夜　　　　　　　　　　　　　林明理

隨之躍起的繁星中　我啣起樹濤聲
久久佇立,以雲遮棚
那曾經飛翔之夢
忽湧到心頭
在柔風中飄動
但我不能劃破這靜謐
在幽思綿綿中
生命已無籲求,我是醒著的

Midnight
Lin Ming-Li

From among the maze of stars   I pick up the sound of tree waves
Standing for long, clouds veiling the shed
The ever dream of flight
Suddenly surging in the mind
Floating in the gentle wind
But I cannot break the silence
In the lingering yearning
Life has no calling; I am awake

🍃 🍃 🍃

48 •

蓮藕花葉圖 吳師道

玉雪皺玲瓏，紛披綠映紅。
生生無限意，只在苦心中。

On the Painting of Lotus Flowers
Wu Shidao

Jade-like and snow-like,
delicate holes in lotus roots;

from among the masses
of green leaves, red bits

& tips are showing and
exhibiting themselves.

Vigor and vitality — in
the bitter heart of lotus seeds.

富源觀景台[15]冥想 　　　　　　　　　林明理

一隻鷹啼叫　忽呦-忽呦
　　　如蒼穹之子,
快要消失卻又躍升 在都蘭灣上。
牠飛入綠野:太陽給牠披上金光。
我東眺遠方島嶼,
　　山巒和海岸寂靜,
　　咸豐草和櫻花都開著。
被藍天和太平洋所圍繞的
　　深淺不一的山影之中,
卑南溪隨著山勢彎延流過。
還有越過青灰色泥岩的山峰的遠處,
我一邊聆聽著燕子和鷹聲,
　　一邊將喜悅對那平原大聲宣告。

Meditation on the Fuyuan Viewing[16] Platform
Lin Ming-Li

An eagle honks, honking-honking
　　Like the son of Heaven,

---

[15] 富源觀景台,位於台東。冬春之際,常有大冠鷲、鳳頭蒼鷹在空中飛翔。觀景平台有360度的環景視野,天晴時,可盡收眼底,美不勝收。

[16] The Fuyuan Viewing Platform is located in the east of Taiwan. During winter and spring, great crowned eagles and crested goshawks are often seen flying and wheeling in the sky. The Viewing Platform boasts a panoramic view of 360 degrees and, when it is fair, everything can be taken into sight; the beauty of the view is boundless.

On the disappearing and to be rising　over Dulan Bay.
It flies into the green field: the sun lends a golden light to it.
I look afar to the distant islands,
　　　The mountains and seashore are silent,
　　　　Xianfeng grass and cherry blossoms are blooming.
Encircled by the blue sky and the Pacific Ocean
　　　　The mountain with different shades of colors,
The Pinan River meanders through the moutains.
And the distant peak through blue-gray mud rock,
I listen to the swallows and eagles,
　While pronouncing my joys.

49 •

風雨圖　　　　　　　　　　　　　　　許衡

南山已見霧昏昏，便合潛身不出門。
直到半途風雨橫，倉皇何處覓前村。

A Scene: Winds & Rains　　　Xu Heng

The southern mountain
is dim and dark, heavy

clouds threatening; it is
advisable to stay home.

Midway, a storm is bursting
in all its fury — I flee hurry-

skurry vainly in search
of a village for a shelter.

元詩明理接千載
古今抒情詩三百首
漢英對照

林田山[17]之歌　　　　　　　　　　　林明理

一條舊鐵道
已不再奔騁於溪谷
當我走近
這山城
早已卸下了嘆息
而風呢喃著
林場的生命故事

Songs of Lintiansan[18]　　　　Lin Ming-Li

An old railway
No longer running through the valleys
When I approach
The mountain city
The sighs have been unloaded
When the wind is whispering
The life story of the forest

50·

登天王台　　　　　　　　　　　　許衡

樓閣荊榛幾變更，登臨祇見古人情。
當年勝跡無人問，依舊春風草又生。

---

[17] 林田山 Lintiensan，位於花蓮縣鳳林鄉的林田山林業文化園區，曾是臺灣的第四大林場。
[18] Lintiansan is located in Lin Tian Shan Forestry Cultural Park, Fenglin Township, Hualien County.

Ascending to the Heavenly Platform

Xu Heng

The pavilion, choked with hazel
and thorns, has been through

many vicissitudes; climbing atop,
only the feelings of ancients

are evoked. Famous historical
sites are ignored, except the green

grass, which grows gradually
when spring wind begins to blow.

淡水紅毛城[19]

林明理

初冬第一個早晨
在古城的中心
在丹麥美人魚的噴水旁
在烏雲挑逗──
空蕩蕩船艙的碼頭旁
這裡
時間緩慢到我幾乎察覺不到細雨在飛
如雪般精緻排列
它主宰了我
讓我可以學會輕鬆以對
然後
隱隱聽見
觀音的微笑慢慢綻開
綿延成島嶼之花

---

[19] 紅毛城，位於臺灣新北市淡水區。

冬藏的莿桐，年年在岸邊眺望
草坪鏽炮上
一座高聳蒼老的
紅毛城
明天是感恩節嗎？
臺北的天空，開始變冷了
我嚐到陽光的慵懶
躲藏在碉堡裡
來回尋找失落的故事
那是介乎綠瓷牆與
這條臺北盆地的母河之間
有著千萬顆忍不住的眼
但只有一聲長嘆
啊，哪裡有我故鄉的夢？
哪裡能夢得見當年居高臨下
露臺的槍眼？
來年又會嚐到什麼，
只有濤濤的河水
嗚咽地流。它嚐到了故鄉的圓月

Tamshui Former British Consulate[20]

Lin Ming-Li

The first morning of early winter
In the center of the old town
By the spraying water of the mermaid of Denmark
Dark clouds flirting —
By the dock with empty cabins

---

[20] Tamshui Former British Consulate is located in Tamsui District of New Taipei City, Taiwan.

Here
Time lingers so I fail to sense the flying drizzles
Such a delicate rank like snow
It dominates me
Let me learn how to deal with it easily
Then
I hear faintly
Guanyin' smile slowly spreading
And extending to be the flowers of the islands
Thorny parasol trees hidden in winter are looking by the bank annually
On the rusty cannon on the grassland
A tall and aged
Tamshui Former British Consulate
Is tomorrow Thanksgiving Day?
The sky of Taibei begins to turn cold
I feel the sun's languidness
It hides itself in the pillbox
In search for the lost tale
Between the green porcelain wall and
That Mother river of Taibei Basin
There are thousands of eyes which cannot bear to see
Yet with only a long sigh
Oh, where is the dream of my hometown?
Where can I dream the past view of overlooking
Of the loopholes of the gazebo?
What would we have in the coming year?
Only the surging river
Is sobbing forward. It tastes the round moon of homeland

🜨 🜨 🜨

51.

宿卓水（其一） 許衡

寒釭挑盡火重生，竹有清聲月自明。
一夜客窗眠不穩，卻聽山犬吠柴荊。

Lodging by the Zhuoshui River (No. 1)
Xu Heng

The cold lamp is spent before
being refueled; clear sound from

the bamboo woods which is
brightened by the bright moon.

The wanderer's window is restless
and sleepless throughout the night,

which is punctuated with the mountain
dog's barking from the wattled door.

遠方傳來的樂音 林明理

像歌詠謬斯的
古希臘詩人一樣
牠，顯得那麼溫柔又帶點憂鬱
那藍紅的翅羽
還有橄欖綠的眼睛
竟唱出一生最美的一曲——愛情
裊裊不絕，如同泉響

Music Wafting From Afar   Lin Ming-Li

Like the ancient Greek poets
Who eulogizes the Muse
He looks so tender and melancholy
The blue-red wings
And the olive-green eyes
Sings the most beautiful song of life — love
Curling and lingering, like a fountain

🌿 🌿 🌿

52 •

宿卓水（其二）   許衡

水自清聲竹有風，我來端欲豁塵蒙。
明朝杖履西城路，悵望家山翠靄中。

Lodging by the Zhuoshui River (No. 2)
Xu Heng

The sound of running water is
clear and clean; I come to wash

off the mortal dust. Tomorrow
morning finds me along the

west road of the town, in straw
sandals and with a walking stick;

looking, melancholy, through
emerald mist, at the native hills.

元詩明理連千載
古今抒情詩三百首
漢英對照

夜航　　　　　　　　　　　　　　　　林明理

是秋的臘染
紫雲，浪潮拍岸
是繁星
旋轉，還有萬重山

當夜敲著故鄉的門
小樓的風鈴就傳開了

那海河的橄欖林
在銀色的石徑裡醒來
被風起的流光
點出滿身晶瑩的背影

只有我於天幕下
仰望高空
在雨濕來臨前
趁著黑夜
飛越玉壁金川……

Night Traveling　　　　　　　　　　Lin Ming-Li

The batik of autumn
Violet clouds, waves beating on the shore
A maze of stars
Spinning, and myriads of mountains

When night knocks on the native door
The wind bell of the small building is jingling

The olive tree by the seas and rivers
Waking up in the silvery stony pathway

The flowing time blown up by the wind
Shines on the shadow with glittering crystals

Only I am standing under the vault of the sky
Looking up
Before the coming of rain
In the dark night
Flying over the jade mountain and golden river…

53．

別友人 　　　　　　　　　　　　　　許衡

永懷不得遂，偃臥惜分陰。
沁北田園計，山東故舊心。

Bidding Adieu to a Friend　　Xu Heng

My long-cherished ambition
failing to be fulfilled, I

seclude myself in my own
room, to cherish the treasured

time. North of the Qinhe River,
the farming plan is planned

carefully; east of the mountain,
my heart lingers on and on.

我倆相識絕非偶然　　　　　　　　　　林明理

如首次展翅而飛的海鷗，
只想與你平行遨遊；
我會努力
絕不輕易墜落…
天空何其寬廣，為自由
我無懼黑暗和險惡，
只想沿著這路到潺潺水流。

Our Meeting Is No Coincidence
Lin Ming-Li

Like the sea dove which flies for the first time,
Just wanting to soar together with you;
I will make efforts
To avoid dropping down easily...
How vast is the sky, and for freedom
I do not dread darkness and danger.
I just want to follow the path to the babbling water.

❀ ❀ ❀

54·

城西遊　　　　　　　　　　劉秉忠

昨朝信馬鳳城西，鞭約垂楊過小堤。
春色滿園花勝錦，黃鸝只揀好枝啼。

Touring the West Town   Liu Bingzhong

Yesterday morning the horse is
free to trot in the west town; a

whip to whip the drooping willows
instead of the horse. Passing the

dyke, a gardenful of spring fair with
flowers more flowery than brocade,

when orioles choose to perch on fair
twigs, to produce melodious notes.

黃昏的福州山   林明理

寒風瑟瑟
周圍是輕拂而過的
蘆葦、花香、鳥鳴
我從未忘記
大台北熟悉的面容
也未曾回避過
生命的每一次悸動

那些年少的純真
忽而被風撩起
啊，朋友
何時再會，一起咀嚼黃昏
當燈火點綴著城市
恰如雨落風過
生活得簡單，蠻好

元詩明理堪千載
古今詩情詩三百首
漢英對照

Dusk on the Fuzhou Mountain

Lin Ming-Li

Chilly wind
Surrounded by flickering
Reeds, floral fragrances, birdsongs
I never forget
The familiar faces of the great Taipei
And I have never avoided
Each throb of life

The innocent youth
Is suddenly brought back by the wind
Oh, my friend
When will we get together to chew the dusk
When the city is dotted with lamps
Like the passing rain and wind
Life is simple, and nice

🌳 🌳 🌳

55 ·

小溪

劉秉忠

小溪流水碧如油，終日忘機羨白鷗。
兩岸桃花春色裡，可能容個釣魚舟。

A Little Creek

Liu Bingzhong

A little creek is running
with water green like oil;

from day to day I forget
the worldly ways, while

admiring the white gulls at
ease. Two bankfuls of peach

flowers are at the height of spring,
where a fishing boat is in motion.

沒有一個海域比得上阿曼灣[21] 林明理

沒有一個海域比得上阿曼灣
　　更讓我深深喜愛；
也沒有任何魚類大得過
　　背部擁有星星的鯨鯊
讓我感到牠的溫柔而掉淚。

這生生不息的水域，
　　讓許多物種不用為生存發愁；
有的沿著海床求偶、產卵
有的話語在潮聲中傳播，
　　是多麼地動人又值得禮讚。

There Is No Sea Like the Gulf of Oman[22]
Lin Ming-Li

There is no sea like the Gulf of Oman
　　Let me deeply love;
And no fish bigger than

---

[21] 阿曼灣是連接阿拉伯海到荷莫茲海峽之間的海域。
[22] The Gulf of Omanis the sea connecting the Arabian Sea and the Hormoz Strait.

A whale shark with a star on its back
For me to feel its tenderness and tears.

This endlessly thriving water,
    For many species not to have to worries about survival;
Some are courting and laying eggs along the seabed
Some words are spreading in the sound of the tide,
    How touching and worthy of praise.

56 ·

溪上   劉秉忠

蘆花遠映釣舟行，漁笛時聞兩三聲。
一陣西風吹雨散，夕陽還在水邊明。

On the Creek   Liu Bingzhong

Among and beyond reed
catkins, a fishing boat is moving

ahead; audible: two or three
piping notes of the fisherman.

Under a spell of west wind,
the rain is scattered and dispelled,

when the setting sun is still
bright over a stretch of water.

春草　　　　　　　　　　　　　林明理

小舟
一如萍藻遊魚
把明窗外的
小橋、亭台
新禾、梯田
都一同蕩漾
在一隻踽步的鷺鷥中
漸遠漸細的是富春江畔

輕風拂過，淺紅淡青
那粉牆黛瓦
隱於畔旁老樹一株
偶來砧杵聲
穿越山林
打起了呆然的回應
該如何想像如何放散而又彌望
竹花枝梗正在凝碧
而我已聽見了　流泉　浪翻

Spring Grass　　　　　　　　　Lin Ming-Li

A small boat
Like a fish through the lakeful of duckweeds
Without the window
Small bridges, kiosks
New crops, terraces
All are poppling together
From a lamely walking egret
By the Fuchun River which is gradually far away

Gentle wind passing, pink red & light green
Red walls and the black tiles
Hidden by an old tree of the bank
Occasional sound of beating clothes
Through mountain forest
Echoing monotonously
How can I imagine and scatter and gaze afar
Bamboo branches & leaves are turning green
I have already heard the running spring and billowing waves

57 ·

三月　　　　　　　　　　　　　　　劉秉忠

背陰花木錦成叢，幽谷鶯啼上苑中。
李白桃紅楊柳綠，天涯無處不春風。

March　　　　　　　　　　　　　Liu Bingzhong

Silk-like clusters of twigs
are flowering in the shade;

orioles, in the deep dale, are
twittering in the imperial

garden. White plums & red
peaches & green willows:

spring wind reaches everywhere — even the horizon.

七月　　　　　　　　　　　　　　　　　　林明理

我橫越過小溪，遠處是
一個映著虹彩的秋塘，
浸沐在雨後明淨的楊樹林
那細碎的苔草前端。

鐘聲緩緩地敲響飄散，
漫過逃離的黃昏；
一棵老樹陷入沉思，
記憶落進流蕩的月光。

我想為你寄書千里，
為你在群山旁隱伏的形象，
以它粗糙的真誠，
載著我和我苦痛的
北方多難的土地；

瞧，那捕捉我們目光的
是黎明前的短暫黑暗－
如果把愛重新點燃
我將再度激起淚水的榮光⋯⋯

July[23]　　　　　　　　　　　　　　　　Lin Ming-Li

I cross the creek, in the distance
An autumn pond mirroring the rainbow

---

[23] Concerning the months, since ancient Chinese poems are written in lunar calendar, in their corresponding English versions, one month is postponed. But in new Chinese poems, the month is exactly translated, as 《七月》 is literally rendered into *July*.

The poplar grove bathed in brightness after rain
Before the fine moss

The sound of bell slowly rings and drifts away
Overflowing the fleeing dusk
An old tree loses itself in deep thought
Memory falls into the waving moonlight

I want to send a letter to you thousands of miles away
For your image hidden in the mountains
With its harsh sincerity
Carrying me and my suffering
Land of north China

Look, what catches our eyes
Is the interim darkness before dawn —
If we kindle love again
Again I will be inspired with the glory of tears…

58 ·

畫鴨　　　　　　　　　　　　　　　　　　揭傒斯

春草細還生，春雛養漸成。
茸茸毛色起，應解自呼名。

Painting of Ducklings　　　　　　　Jie Xisi

Spring grass, fair and
fine, undergoes birth

and rebirth; ducklings
are gradually growing,

to be grown: downy and
fluffy — quack, quack,

quack — they seem to
be calling their own name.

妳是一條聖光的溪流—致倫札・阿涅利

林明理

在古城和沉思的海岸間，
我小小的夢漫遊著。我喜愛
遨遊西西里島遠甚其他之地，
所以沿它的老路走，我將
憩止於內布羅迪山脈之一隅，
猶如乘著一彎彩虹，橫跨時空，
我想唱給妳聽，噢，美麗的倫札，
——雲和天，第勒尼安海。
在那山海之間，
妳，恰似一條聖光的溪流。

You Are a Stream of Sacred Light — to Renza Agnelli

Lin Ming-Li

Between the old town and the brooding shore,
My little dream is wandering. I love —
Travelling to Sicily more than other places,
So following its old path, I will
Rest in a corner of the Nebrodi Mountains,
Like riding a rainbow, across time and space,
I want to sing to you, O beautiful Renza,

— The clouds and the sky, the Tyrrhenian Sea.
Among the mountains and the seas,
You are like a stream of sacred light.

❀ ❀ ❀

59 •

寒夜作 揭傒斯

疏星凍霜空,流月濕林薄。
虛館人不眠,時聞一葉落。

Inspired on a Cold Night Jie Xisi

Sparse stars against
the frozen frosty sky;

the moon is flowing
over the moist thin forest.

An empty hotel houses a
sleep-deprived wanderer,

who hears the falling of a
single leaf — now, and then.

可仍記得 林明理

好想走出窗外
直駛到海灣的心裡去

在另一片秋雲下
掠過一葉一葉的歸帆

可仍記得
帶著微吟的流泉
繞過我的彌望
暮霞也漸隱杳然

當漁火，溫煦的，彩繪波紋
我，已停止每一分的波動
那只是個富麗的溫柔
仍守在無重力的時空

Do You Still Remember Lin Ming-Li

I really want to go out of the window
Straight into the heart of the bay
Under another piece of autumn cloud
Skimming through one after another leaf of returning sail

Do you still remember
The spring with a gentle babbling
Around my expectation
The twilight clouds gradually fade away

When the fishing light, warm, painted ripples
I have stopped every minute of waving
It is just a rich tenderness
Still in the weightless space-time

60.

秋雁 揭傒斯

寒向江南暖,饑向江南飽。
莫道江南惡,須道江南好。

Migratory Wild Geese   Jie Xisi

When it is cold,
the migratory wild

geese fly southward
for warmth; when

hungry, they fly south-
ward for food. Speak

not ill of the south,
which is fair and fine.

獨白 林明理

如果可以
我想在妳心底
搭一座機會的橋
漏出了一線明亮的
天藍

罄
與鈸——
迴繞著遠樹
倒映這岩上的積雪

直是靈隱深處的
佛音

啊,若能化曉鐘
叩門,心湖也留下妳
珍藏的情真,我便
以山的俯視
和海的低唱
踏浪飛回……

Soliloquy   Lin Ming-Li

If it is possible
In your heart I want to
Build a bridge of opportunity
Revealing a bright ray of
Sky-blue

Stone drums
And cymbals —
Around the remote trees
Reflecting the snow on the rock
Simply the voice of Buddhism from the depth
Of the soul

Oh, if I can be transformed into a morning bell
Knocking at the door, the lake of heart will keep you
The treasured feeling, and I
Looking up as a mountain
And the murmuring of the sea
Riding the waves, to fly back……

🌳 🌳 🌳

61·

題信上人春蘭秋蕙二首（其二）   揭傒斯

幽叢不盈尺，空谷為誰芳？
一徑寒雲色，滿林秋露香。

Two Inscriptions on the Painting by a Monk-Friend (No. 2)   Jie Xisi

Small secluded clusters
of flowers — in such an

empty valley, for whom to
be fragrant? A path veiled

with cold clouds, and
the forest is filled with

autumn dew, emanating
spells of sweet scent.

如果   林明理

如果
僅有一片窗可供祝禱：
我願與你並肩
   坐在陽光角隅
為世界而歌。

你的喜笑與沉默
以詩的形式

同繪畫結合[24]
充滿希望
　與生命的壯闊；

而我不曾懷疑過
　真理，
因為無論時間如何流轉
　世上所有的幸福
都因有你而向我微笑。

If　　　　　　　　　　　　　　　Lin Ming-Li

If
There were only one window for prayer:
I would sit side by side with you
　In a sunny corner
To sing for the world.

Your laughter and silence
In the form of poetry[25]
　Combined with painting
Full of hope
　And the grandeur of life;

And I have never doubted
　The truth,
Because no matter how the time goes
　All the happiness in the world
Smiles to me because of you.

---

[24] 2024 年 9 月 16 日週一 PROF. ERNESTO KAHAN 電郵給明理他的畫作，因而為詩。

[25] On Monday, September 16, 2024, Professor Ernesto Kahan emailed Ming-Li his painting, hence the poem.

62 ·

女兒浦歌二首（其二） 揭傒斯

大孤山前女兒灣，大孤山下浪如山。
山前日日風和雨，山下舟船自往還。

Two Poems on the Daughter Bay (No. 2)
Jie Xisi

Before the Great Lonely Mountain
is the Daughter Bay; beneath

the Great Lonely Mountain
the waves are surging mountain-

high. The mountain is caught,
from day to day, in howling winds

& lashing rains, when the boats are
journeying to and fro in great ease.

愛的讚歌 林明理

藍色冰湖上
兩隻寒鴨
腳蹼快速拍動
彼此相伴，輕輕
掠過白樺林

多麼靜好
令人羨煞

就像愛情
來得奇妙
當它來時
仍會迫不及待
仍會理解那份激動
就像獨行荒野中
採擷一小串鵝莓
孩子般的
手舞足蹈

啊,只有它
無論黑夜或白天
永遠不息
又有誰能詮釋
它的面容
或滄桑
或最美的樣子

The Hymn of Love   Lin Ming-Li

On the blue ice lake
Two cold ducks
Quickly flipping their fins
Together, gently
Passing through the birch forest
So nice and quiet
So enviable

Like love
Which comes so wonderfully

When it comes
You burst with impatience
And understandable excitement
Like walking alone in the wilderness
To pick a cluster of gooseberries
And dance
Like a child

Oh only it
Night or day
Never stops
Who can interpret
Its face
Or vicissitudes
Or its beauty itself

63 •

雲錦溪棹歌五首（其五）   揭傒斯

溪上層層雲錦山，垂楊盡處是龍灘。
不是孤舟來逆上，何人知道世途難。

Five Boating Songs (No. 5)   Jie Xisi

Over the creek layers upon
layers of silver- & silk-lined

clouds; the end of the drooping
willows is nursing the Dragon

Beach. Without a lonely boat
boating against the current,

who knows the difficulties
of the worldly ways?

為雨林而歌　　　　　　　　　林明理

那片剛果盆地森林
藏有許多
秘密。

許多巴卡族人及生物得以
生存
上萬年，有些誤闖者
只能跋涉，勉強生存數日。

有大貓等動物　漫走在
大荒野，有數十億顆樹
挺立在泥灰沼澤；如同某些
無法預測又令人驚奇的事物。

創造者守護著這一切，
盜獵者的砍伐和破壞
在哭泣的天空下。

而我不想僅僅是這麼說：

雨林是有記憶的，它的聲音
是天使的笛聲…
也可以是憂傷的。

In Praise of the Rain Forest   Lin Ming-Li

The Congo Basin Forest
Holds many
Secrets.

Many Baka and creatures have survived
For tens of thousands of years, and some trespassers
Can barely survive for a few days by trekking.

There are cats and other animals roaming
The great moors, and billions of trees
Standing in marl bogs; like something
Unpredictable and amazing.

The Creator guards it all,
The poachers cut and destroy
Under the crying sky.

And I don't want to just say:

The rainforest has a memory, its voice
Is the fluting of an angel…
It can also be sorrowful.

64 ·

和歐陽南陽月夜思   揭傒斯

月出照中園，鄰家猶未眠。
不嫌風露冷，看到樹陰圓。

In Reply to Ouyang Nanyang on a Moonlit Night
Jie Xisi

A bright moon rises
to shine over the court-

yard, whose neighbor
is still awake. Dreading

no cold wind and
dew, watching and

admiring, until the shade
of the tree is round.

從海邊回來
林明理

悠悠淡淡，晚歸的星
溜上冬青樹，風
拎著裙擺，沿著槐花巷
從黃牆的寺院跑回
隨鐘鼓，輕輕一敲
簷滴聲
不斷

幾隻舢舨，白濤閃耀
碎在浪峰的盡頭
在那被吹得彎彎的
平灘上，看見自己
影子的延展
伸到蒼海
又落在腳前

紅燈點點,葉灑石階
我是羞藏在夜露裡的綠草
告訴我
那八萬四千的詩偈
隨風低吟
是否也淌進遊子的心田
燃起另一種慈悲?

Back From the Sea   Lin Ming-Li

Leisurely and light, the late star
Slip onto the Holly tree, the wind
Carrying the skirt, along the pagoda flower lane
To be back from the yellow wall of the temple
With the bell drum, a gentle knock
And the eaves drip
constantly

A few sampans, the white waves shining
Breaking at the end of the waves
On the blown flat beach
To see their shadows
Stretching out
To the pale sea
And falling at their feet

The red light is flashing, leaves falling on the stone steps
I am the shy green grass hidden in the night dew
Tell me
The eighty-four thousand verses
Whisper in the wind
Are they flowing into the wanderer's heart
To ignite another kind of compassion?

65・

蘇台竹枝詞 　　　　　　　　　楊維楨

楊柳青青楊柳黃，青黃變色過年光。
妾似柳絲易憔悴，郎如柳絮太顛狂。

Song of Bamboo Branch 　　Yang Weizhen

The willows are green, and
the willows are yellow; with

the alternation of green and
yellow, a year after another year

is spent. Like the willow twig,
it is easy for me to be emaciated,

while, like willow catkins, you
are crazy and wild as a libertine.

靜靜的岱山湖 　　　　　　　　林明理

靜靜的岱山湖，
如拉斐爾手繪的聖母。
人在畫中走，
綠是一種顏色。
那裡群峰疊翠，出塵不染。
那裡清波蕩漾，荷影招展
在粧點華美的小舟上。

我凝神看了又看，
啊，就這樣——
放慢了腳步，依偎著繆斯笑了。

The Quiet Daishan Lake   Lin Ming-Li

The quiet Daishan Lake,
Like Madonna hand-painted by Raphael.
People walk in the painting,
Green is a color.
Where the peaks are piled green, the dust is not stained.
There are clear waves, with lotus flowers blossoming
On the colorfully decorated boat.
I look and look again,
Ah, that's it —
Steps slowing down, snuggling up to the Muse with a smile.

66 ·

繡   楊維楨

揀得金針出象筒，鴛鴦雙刺扇羅中。
卻嗔昨夜狸奴惡，抓亂金床五色絨。

Embroidery   Yang Weizhen

Out of the trinket box she
carefully chooses a golden needle;

a pair of mandarin ducks are
being embroidered on the fine

texture of the fan. A great pity:
last night it is spoiled by the

palm civet, who has scrambled
and jumbled the five colors.

簡靜是美 林明理

偶爾
還是會坐在窗前奇想
毫不以深秋
為意
大發詩興
上臨且無聲的
星子將離城隱入雲影的背後
銀霧牽著一彎新月
推開林叢的門,漫步
老年山坡
而我
不由自主地
探頭
旁聽
涼風看守著
蟲兒們的合奏
凝結的天容也撼動

Quiet Is Beauty Lin Ming-Li

Occasionally
Still sitting at the window wondering
Not to take late autumn
Seriously
Poetically inspired

Upward and silent
Stars will leave the city, to be hidden into the shadow of the clouds
The silvery fog holding a crescent moon
To open the door of the forest, walking
Along the old hillside
And I
Involuntarily
Probe
To listen to
The cool wind watching
The ensemble of the insects
Condensation of the day also shaken

🍃 🍃 🍃

67 ·

題春江漁父圖   楊維楨

一片青天白鷺前，桃花水泛住家船。
呼兒去換城中酒，新得槎頭縮項鯿。

Poem on the Painting   Yang Weizhen

Against a patch of blue sky,
white egrets are sailing.

Peach flowers blossoming,
a fishing boat is tethered

by the shore. The fisherman
asks his son to buy wine

from the town, the freshly
caught bream as the tip.

冬日湖畔的柔音　　　　　　　　　　林明理

牠直挺挺地佇立在低枝上，
對林中的眾鳥毫不在意，
只靜靜地聆聽小山丘呢喃，
享受著各種溫度的幸福。
人們傳說中的愛的禱語
如清風，直抵
陽光下綿延的小徑。
而我獨自閒蕩，
輕盈，欣喜──
宛若拂草的蝴蝶，
不留下任何足跡。

The Soft Music by the Winter Lake
　　　　　　　　　　　　　　Lin Ming-Li

The bird stands upright on a low branch,
And it pays no attention to the other birds in the woods,
Only listening to the whispers from the small hill,
Enjoying the various shades of happiness.
The legendary prayer of love
Like gentle breeze, coming
To the sun-bathed trail.
As I wander alone,
Light-hearted, filled with joy ─
The butterfly shadow whisks across the grass,
Without leaving any footprint.

68．

墨梅　　　　　　　　　　　　　　　　王冕

我家洗硯池頭樹，朵朵花開淡墨痕。
不要人誇顏色好，只留清氣滿乾坤。

Plum Flowers in Ink　　　　　　　Wang Mian

The trees by the inkslab-
washing pond are darkish

with inky blossoms after
blossoms. No need to be

flattered with their flaring
color, only wishing to fill

the universe with their air
which is pure and clean.

茂林紫蝶幽谷[26]　　　　　　　　　　林明理

每年冬天
　數十萬隻紫蝶遠渡重洋
如一群小精靈來到大武山腳下
　溫暖靜謐的山谷。

當雲霧被第一道晨光喚醒，
　枝椏密葉中鳥聲清脆。

---

[26] 高雄茂林紫蝶幽谷，和太平洋彼端的墨西哥「帝王斑蝶谷」，併列為全世界僅有的兩處大規模的「越冬型蝶谷」。

牠們一圈圈旋舞、輕盈飄然,
　採集蜜源食草。

牠們在陽光裡追逐,
　高高低低地滑行,
　時而停歇在花間草浪,
　　直到春天才陸續離開。

千百年來
每年冬天在這裡重複的演出,
構成了地球上最美麗的史詩。

Maolin Purple Butterflies Valley[27]

Lin Ming-Li

Each winter
Hundreds of thousands of purple butterflies cross the ocean
Like fairies to the warm and quiet valley
At the foot of Dawu Mountain.

When the clouds are awakened by the first light of morning,
The birds sing in the branches and leaves.
They dance in circles and gently fly about,
Gathering nectar and while eating grass.

They chase in the sun,
Glide high and low,
And sometimes stop in flowers or grassy waves,
Until the coming spring before leaving one after another.

---

[27] Maolin Purple Butterflies Valley in Kaohsiung and the Monarch Butterflies Valley in Mexico on the other side of the Pacific Ocean are listed as the only two large-scale "overwintering butterflies valleys" in the world.

For thousands of years
The performances repeated here each winter,
To constitute the most beautiful epic on the earth.

69 •

梅花　　　　　　　　　　　　　　王冕

三月東風吹雪消，湖南山色翠如澆。
一聲羌笛無人見，無數梅花落野橋。

Plum Blossoms　　　　　　Wang Mian

The east wind of April blows
away the snow; the mountain

color south of the lake is
splashing emerald. A few

fluting notes without listeners;
countless plum blossoms,

dropping and falling, on
and across the wild bridge.

武陵農場風情　　　　　　　　林明理

立春後，一大片粉紅，耀眼的櫻花
　　充盈在枝葉交錯的山谷中。
我像是迷了路般緩緩前行，

這些古老的神木群棧道，──
傳來風聲，鳥聲與流水聲。

哦，聳入雲霄的山頂，澄明的天空，
　果樹和花卉全都浪漫而生氣勃勃。
在瞭望台下，在群山屏障下，
　周遭都寂靜。只有瀑布聲
　　似遠又近地在我耳邊唱響。

哦，多清澈的七家灣溪呀，
從大甲溪上游，越過神聖的稜線…
　　…來到這狹長形山谷。
而我聽到櫻花鉤吻鮭來回游動的聲音，
多麼欣喜，又是多麼地令人動容。

Kaleidoscope of Wuling Farm

Lin Ming-Li

After the start of spring, a large field of pink, dazzling cherry blossoms
Fill the valley with branches and leaves.
I walk slowly, as if lost,
These ancient sacred wood group trestle road —
Comes the sound of wind, birds and water.

Oh, the soaring peaks, the clear sky,
The fruit trees and flowers are all romantic and lively.
Beneath the lookout, beneath the walls of the mountains,
Everything is silent. Only the sound of the waterfall
Seems to sing in my ears from afar and near.
Oh, how clear Qijiawan Stream is,
From the upper reaches of Dajia Stream, across the sacred prism…
…Coming to this narrow valley.

And I hear the sound of Formosan Landlocked Salmon
swimming back and forth,
How joyful, and how moving.

❦ ❦ ❦

70 ·

白梅　　　　　　　　　　　　　　　　王冕

冰雪林中著此身，不同桃李混芳塵。
忽然一夜清香發，散作乾坤萬里春。

White Plum Blossoms　　　　　Wang Mian

Planted in the forest of ice and
snow; white plum blossoms are

different from peaches and apricots
which grow out of the earth. A

sudden gust of sweet scent throughout the night, which is dispersing

and suffusing the heaven and
earth: myriads of miles of spring.

永懷學者詩人楊牧[28]　　　　　　　林明理

天上的星啊，和你一樣
在銀河中舞

---

[28] 楊牧老師辭世於 2020 年 3 月 13 日，享壽八十，曾任教於美國、東華大學文學院等校；一生獲得殊榮無數，值得尊崇。

你源自花蓮
那兒有朵朵浪花
眾鳥遨翔在縱谷和山巒
有你的詩情把夜空填滿
有你的夢想和太平洋的呼喚

你從銀河的北面奔向故鄉
立在七星潭一側
草海桐默默，四周是歌聲，緩緩
而你溫文的眼神
如晨星，平靜如深潭
迎接無限的陽光
健步登上了永恆的天堂

Eternal Memory of Yang Mu[29] As a Poet-Scholar
Lin Ming-Li

O stars in the sky, like you
Dance in the Milky Way
You come from Hualien
Where there are waves upon waves
The birds fly in the valleys and mountains
And your poetry fills the night sky
Your dreams and the call of the Pacific

You run from the north of the Milky Way to your hometown
Standing on the side of the Seven Star Pool
Naupaka is silent, surrounded by singing, slowly

---

[29] Yang Mu passed away on March 13, 2020, at the age of 80. He has ever taught in the United States and Donghua University. He enjoyed a lifetime of honors and respect.

And your gentle eyes
Like the morning star, calm as a deep pool
To meet the infinite sunshine
Briskly walking into the eternal heaven

71.

梅花（其六）　　　　　　　　　　王冕

老幹漬清霜，寒梢掛新月。
徐徐暗香來，可是春機泄？

Plum Blossoms (No. 6)　　　Wang Mian

Old branches,
gnarled, are steeped

in pure frost; cold
treetops, a new moon

is hanging. Hidden
scent is slowly wafting

here: is the secret
of spring divulged?

在思念的夜裡　　　　　　　　　　林明理

啊，我遠方的友人像朵白色小雛菊，
悄悄綻放在西西里島一隅；

一天又一天，
她的生活以及眼裡盡是詩意。

啊，她一旁的丈夫和孩子笑得多甜蜜，
我親愛的倫扎，卻與我相隔千里；
一天又一天，
除了從太平洋望出去，在思念的夜裡。

所有山巒都在守望，小河也唱起了歌謠，
而我把一束滿綴星鑽的雲隙光送給妳⋯
一天又一天，
直到妳驚奇地發現：它如花般明亮聖潔。

-2024.9.17

In the Night of Longing   Lin Ming-Li

Ah, my friend afar is like a little white daisy,
Which blooms quietly in a corner of Sicily;
Day after day,
Her life and her eyes are filled with poetry.

Oh, how sweetly her husband and children smile beside her,
My dear Renza is a thousand miles away;
Day after day,
Except looking out from the Pacific Ocean, in the night of longing.

All the mountains are watching, all the rivers are singing,
And I send you a beam of star-studded cloudy light….
Day after day,
Until you are surprised to find: it is as bright and holy as a flower.

September 17, 2024

72.

過濟源登裴公亭　　　　　　耶律楚材

山接青霄水浸空，山光灩灩水溶溶。
風回一鏡揉藍淺，雨過千峰潑黛濃。

Passing Jiyuan and Climbing Peigong Pavilion
　　　　　　　　　　　　　　Yelü Chucai

The blue mountains dissolve in the clouds where the sky is dipped in

water; the mountains are resplendent and the waters are rippling. The

wind is kissing a mirror which is light blue and the rain, splattering

and sputtering across myriads of mountains, is splashing heavy ink.

時光裡的和平島[30]　　　　　　　林明理

為了愛，我又回來
你，純淨無邪的野百合
在回憶的波上
在我嚮往已久的岸邊踱步唱歌

---

[30] 和平島是離臺灣最近的離島，位於基隆港北端、港口東側。

高山阻擋不了你的魅力
峽谷隱藏不了你的柔情
河流帶不走你的憂鬱
大海為你永遠守誓

聽，金風蕭瑟，塵海起伏
那飛逝的季節裡
你仍是你
無懼驚世駭俗

多少冬夏與春秋
多少痛苦或歡笑
我愛你，天然的模樣
愛你不用讀唇的細語

今夜，我是詩人
我看到了鷗鳥從岸畔飛起
瞬時，浪花有了節奏
隨你起伏跌宕

當月兒停坐在尖石上
聆聽浪濤時
你的光芒湧動
而時間過去了

光的細鱗在你四周
你的美麗
已戰勝了腐朽
秋波渺渺，暮靄重重

你像玉山剛下的雪
白而光明

而我在懸崖的寧靜中
呼喚你,從這裡到光的盡頭

The Island of Peace in Time[31]   Lin Ming-Li

For love, I come back
You, pure and innocent wild lily
On the waves of memory
Are pacing the shore of my longing for a long time while singing

The mountains fail to stop your charm
The canyons cannot hide your tenderness
The rivers cannot take away your melancholy
The sea forever keeps the oath for you

Listen, the golden wind is bleak, the dust sea undulating
In the fleeting season
You are still you
Not afraid of the world

How many winter, summer, spring and autumn
How much pain or laughter
I love you, the natural way
I love your whispers instead of reading lips

Tonight, I am a poet
I saw gulls flying from the shore
In an instant, the waves are with a rhythm
Ups and downs with you

---

[31] The Island of Peace is the closest outlying island to Taiwan, located at the north end and east side of Keelung Port.

When the moon sits on the sharp stone
Listening to the waves
Your light is surging
And time is sliding by

The scales of light are all around you
Your beauty
Has triumphed over the decay
Boundless are autumn waves, dusk mist upon mist

You are as white and bright as
The snow freshly falling in the jade mountain
And in the silence of the cliff, I
Call you, from here to the end of the light

🌳 🌳 🌳

73 ·

過天山和上人韻二絕（其一） 耶律楚材

從征萬里走風沙，南北東西總是家。
落得胸中空索索，凝然心是白蓮花。

In Reply to a Monk-Friend Yelü Chucai

Trekking through myriads
of miles of windy sand:

north or south, east
or west, home is anywhere.

The mind is empty,
at a great loss, and the

heart, stable and steady,
is a white pond lily.

山韻 　　　　　　　　　　　　　　　　林明理

我說
我聽見了樹與星群齊舞的足音
你說
那是大雁在煙波細雨中
急急緩緩　　往雲裡行

我說
我看見了千燈閃爍於萬巒峰頂
你說
那是流螢帶著清涼的鈴鐺
飛過原野　飛過沼澤　飛往自由的天庭

啊，這才想起
那杉林溪的風　　施豆肥的老農
從心的隙縫
停泊在離我不遠的斜坡之地
霧還沒褪盡　　蟲聲落滿胸懷

The Charm of the Mountain　　Lin Ming-Li

I say
I have heard the footfall of trees and stars
You say
They are the wild geese sailing in
mist and fog now slowly and then swiftly

I say
I have seen thousands of lamps flashing in myriads of mountains
You say
They are the flowing fireflies with cool bells
Flying over fields and marshes, into the free paradise

Ah, so to remember
The wind of the brook of firs   the old fertilizing farmer
From the rift of the heart
Anchoring on the slope not far away
The fog still lingering   insects chirping fills my bosom

74 •

懷親二首（其二） 耶律楚材

黃沙三萬里，白髮一孀親。
腸斷邊城月，徘徊照旅人。

Longing for My Relative   Yelü Chucai

Yellow sands through
three thousand miles;

a widow-relative who
is white-crowned. Heart-

broken is the moon
hanging over the border

town, which is lingering
& shining on the wanderer.

寒風吹起 　　　　　　　　　　　　　　　林明理

鬱鬱的，冬在怯怯萌芽
遠處幾聲犬號，擊破四周靜默
請聽，風的狂野曲調
草原都迷失在初雪中
在清曠的夜色
我想吟哦
浮光底下
多少尋尋覓覓的憧憬
恍然清醒
無聲的落入大海
波瀾也不起了
這鴻飛如旅人的，那裡來的
江南之雪喲
你或已忘記？請聽風在舞踴
當一切都靜止下來，卻盡夠使
我感到清寒，那無數的
瞬間，織就成綿密的鄉愁
向澄澄的明月，羣山紛紛白頭

When Cold Wind Blows 　　　　Lin Ming-Li

Depressed, winter is budding timidly
A few dogs barking from far away, breaking the enveloping silence
Please listen, the wind's wild melody
The grassland lost in the early snow
In the cool vastness of the night
I want to sing

Under the floating light
How many seekings, longings, and expectations
Sudden realization
Noiselessly falling into the sea
Even without waves
The flight is like the snow of the south,
from a traveler

Have you forgotten? Please listen to the dancing of the wind
When everything comes to a still, enough
For me to feel the cold freshness, the countless
Instants, woven into thick and dense nostalgia
Towards the clear moon, the mountains, one by one, are all
white-crowned

🌳 🌳 🌳

75 ·

夜坐彈離騷　　　　　　　　　　　耶律楚材

一曲離騷一椀茶，個中真味更何加。
香銷燭燼窮廬冷，星斗闌幹山月斜。

Night Sitting & Playing *The Parting Sorrow*
Yelü Chucai

A piece of music from
The Parting Sorrow and

a bowl of tea — what taste
is more tasty, and more

tasteful? Joss sticks burnt,
candle spent, the room cold

— the stars sparse, and the
mountain moon shining aslant.

流星雨　　　　　　　　　　　　　　　林明理

你是一把散滿霜風的
北望的弓，那颼颼的箭
射下　簾外泣零的雪

The Meteor Shower　　　　　　Lin Ming-Li

You are a bow looking north
in a frosty wind, the whizzing arrow
shooting down　the weeping snow beyond the curtain

🌳 🌳 🌳

76 ·

洞山五位頌　　　　　　　　　　　　耶律楚材

區區遊子困風塵，就路還家觸處真。
芳草滿川桃李亂，風光全似故園春。

The Field Scenery　　　　　　　Yelü Chucai

A wanderer is wandering
alone along the way,

which takes him home.
The field is filled

with sweet grass, as
well as peaches and

apricots — the scenery
is that of native land.

春日的玉山   林明理

美麗的朝霞
在遠離陸地的海面上
緊緊跟隨它的
是忠實的太陽
青青草上露珠
依戀地打濕了褲管
而我專注地，凝視東方
啊，無邊的黑夜
啊，無邊的海洋
還有無數個對愛嚮往的心

是不是
如我深情眺望
它像老鷹一樣沉著而安詳
是不是
像一朵百合在開放
那第一道晨曦般閃動的光
是不是
如自由的標誌
像母親
守護襁褓般堅強

元詩明理撼千載
古今抒情詩三百首
漢英對照

啊,遠遠的
遠遠的
那微笑的黎明
似乎在告訴我
該把痛苦輕輕地釋放
在空曠中
再沒有
那毫不相稱的輕狂
有的只是
我感覺一陣輕微的悸動

想不到
它美麗而龐大的
生命裡竟貯藏了這麼多芬芳
讓我眼淚無法再次隱藏
它那繆斯沉默般的眼神
教我不再彷徨
這或許是它
在無盡的岸邊甜美的呼喚
到如今,我的愛猶然迴響
烙在與島嶼相連的玉山

The Jade Mountain in Spring Lin Ming-Li

The beautiful morning clouds
At the sea far from the land
Closely following up
Is the loyal sun
Dewdrops on the green grass
Lingering to wet the trousers
Yet with concentration, I gaze on the east
Oh, endless night

Oh, boundless sea
And innumerable hearts longing for love

Is it so
Like my affectionate looking afar
As calm and sedate as an eagle
Is it so
Like a lily blossoming
The first twinkling light in the dawn
Is it so
Like the sign of freedom
Like the mother
Strong when she is guarding her baby

Oh, far away
Far away
The smiling dawn
Seems to be telling me
The pain should be relieved
In the open
No more
That indifferent frivolity
What is left is only
A feeling of slight throb

Unexpectedly
In the grand and beautiful life
So much fragrance is contained
My tears, no way to be concealed again
The expression in its eyes like the Muse
Teaching me to hesitate no more
Maybe it is
A sweet calling from the boundless shore
Up till now, my love is still echoing
Carved on the Jade Mountain connecting the islands

元詩明理瑧千載
古今詩情詩三百首
漢英對照

77·

透脫不透脫　　　　　　　　　　耶律楚材

重陽九日菊花新，妙契忘言不犯春。
收得安南憂伐北，不知何日得通津。

When the Port Is Open to Navigation?
Yelü Chucai

Chrysanthemums are fresh
on the Double Ninth Day —

so wonderful that words
are spared for the beauty

of spring. The southern land
recovered, northern expedition

is schemed — when the
port is open to navigation?

與菊城開封相會　　　　　　　　　林明理

菊城裡
我像一隻喜鵲
兜著圈子
唱歌。

時近重陽
夜裡

我從菊白堆裡撈出
　一首詩。

當殿前菊燈齊放
溫潤了老城
月傾斜，莫名的靜
撫慰著人心。

Meeting in Kaifeng as a City of Chrysanthemums
　　　　　　　　　　　　　　　Lin Ming-Li

In the city of chrysanthemums
Like a magpie
I am circling and
Singing

The Double Ninth Day approaching
In the night
I fish out a poem
From the pile of white chrysanthemums

When the chrysanthemum lamps before the temple are on
To warm and moisten the old city
The moon slanting, queer quiet
Soothes the heart.

🍀 🍀 🍀

三月廿日題所寓屋壁　　　　　　　倪瓚

梓樹花開破屋東，鄰牆花信幾番風。
閉門睡過兼旬雨，春事依依是夢中。

元詩明理媲千載
古今詩憶詩三百首
漢英對照

Inscription on the Wall   Ni Tsan

Catalpa flowers are blossoming
against the eastern house;

the adjacent walls are blown
in winds and tides of news

of flowering. Sleeping behind
the closed door, through

raining for ten days, spring
is lingering in a fond dream.

寒冬過後   林明理

在荒野的路途上，
周圍有渡鴨啼鳴
黎明姍姍來遲
但山風清涼。
一隻灰熊
饑餓地尋找食物，
麋鹿、狼群、美洲豹等
隱隱出沒。
當陽光照亮了
整個山脈，
啊，大自然的一切
就是一種純然的喜悅。

After the Winter   Lin Ming-Li

In the wilderness,
There are ducks squawking around

The day dawns slowly
The mountain wind is cool
A hungry gray bear
Is looking for food
Elks, wolves, leopards....
Appearing now and then
When the sun shines
On the entire mountain,
Oh, everything in nature
Is a kind of pure joy

79·

晚照軒偶題 倪瓚

簷前幽鳥自相呼，池上紅藻映綠蒲。
五月夜涼如八月，一窗風雨夢南湖。

An Impromtu Ni Tsan

Before the eaves the birds
are calling and pleasing each

other; over the pond red lotus
flowers are setting off green

sedges. In June the night is
cool like that of September;

a windowful of winds & rains,
a dream of the south lake.

元詩明理邁千載
古今抒情詩三百首
漢英對照

默禱   林明理

1.
主啊,請聽我看我,
我用心歌唱,隨行左右。

2.
我多麼渺小,
如一粒霜雪,故無所求。

3.
瞧,岩石海底,白鯨洄游⋯
領受祢的恩典與巧思。

4.
唯我,始終站得筆直,
冬盡春來,幾個秋。

5.
噢,主啊,我邊看極地之花,
邊朝祢走去,這就是我——
幸福的定格。

Silent Prayer   Lin Ming-Li

1.
Lord, please listen to me and look at me,
I sing with my heart, and follow you wherever you go.

2.
How small I am,
Like a grain of frosty snow, which has nothing to desire.

3.
Lo, at the rocky bottom, white whales are swimming back⋯
To receive your grace and ingenuity.

4.
I am the only one who always stands upright,
Winter gone, spring coming, and a few autumns.

5.
Oh, my Lord, while looking at polar flowers,
I walk toward you, this is me —
The freezing frame of happiness.

🌳 🌳 🌳

80 •

客舍詠牽牛花 倪瓚

小盤承露淨鉛華，玉露依稀染碧霞。
弱質幽姿娛我老，傍人籬落蔓秋花。

The Morning Glory   Ni Tsan

Small plates contain dew which
purifies all; the crystal dew is

faintly dyed in colorful clouds.
With the morning glory's weak

stems and graceful sprawling,
I am delighted as an old man;

autumn flowers are lingering
and clinging against the hedges.

緬懷山寺之音
　　　　　　　　　　　　　　　　林明理

離開山寺已多年
而此刻，誦經聲起
我沐浴光明
再一次體驗感情的波動

我擁有的，只是儉樸之道
我所眷戀的塵世，遺忘了也好
我找尋，找尋寧靜——
終於被一顆星引導，來到佛的路

在木魚聲聲、八塔的佛寺中
我重遊了這舊地……
……那闊別已久的思念
使我像草葉上的露珠般顫動

林明理畫　　　　　　　佛光山

Memory of the Sound of Mountains & Temples
　　　　　　　　　　　　　　Lin Ming-Li

It has been many years since I left the temple
At this moment, there is the chanting
I am bathed in light
Once again to experience the fluctuations of emotions

All I have is a simple way
The mortal world I love, if forgotten, ok
I am in search of peace —
Finally to be led by a star, to the path of Buddha

In the sound of wooden fish and the Buddhist temple of
eight pagodas
I revisited the old place....
...The thought of long absence
Makes me quiver like the dew on a blade of grass

81 ·

吳仲圭山水　　　　　　　　　　　　　　倪瓚

道人家住梅花村，窗下松醪滿石樽。
醉後揮毫寫山色，嵐霏雲氣淡無痕。

The Landscape of Hills and Rills Ni Tsan

A Taoist lives in the village of
plum blossoms, beneath whose

window a stone bottle is filled
with loose mash as a kind of liquor.

Tipsy, he wields his brush smartly
to paint a landscape painting,

where the mountains are veiled in
clouds scudding away to be traceless.

元詩明理撐千載
古今抒情詩三百首
漢英對照

重歸自然　　　　　　　　　林明理

這一片淺水海域
孕育出的野外天堂，
蝴蝶、小動物和鳥
充滿著多彩季節的旋律。

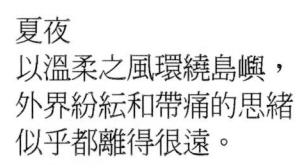

夏夜
以溫柔之風環繞島嶼，
外界紛紜和帶痛的思緒
似乎都離得很遠。

只有圓月在林梢慢移，
而我的心
也在尋求重歸自然
——寧靜的聲音。

Lin Mingli / painting

Return to Nature　　　　　Lin Ming-Li

This shallow water sea area
Has bred a wild paradise
Butterflies, small animals and birds
Full of colorful seasonal melody.

Summer night
Gentle winds embrace the island,
The chaotic world and painful thoughts
Seem to be so far away.

Only the moon is slowly moving at the top of the forest,
And my heart
Tries to return to nature
— A quiet voice.

82 •

偶成　　　　　　　　　　　　　　　　　倪瓚

紫燕低飛不動塵，黃鸝嬌小未勝春。
東風綠遍門前草，暮雨寒煙愁殺人。

An Impromptu　　　　　　　　　　　Ni Tsan

The swallows are flying low,
without raising any dust; yellow

orioles, tenderly small, add
a finishing touch to the fair

spring. The east wind is greening
the grass before the door, when

the misty rain at dusk brings
sorrow to the watcher-wanderer.

妝點秋天　　　　　　　　　　　　　　林明理

古老的山陵和海線，
這福爾摩沙的指環⋯
⋯撩撥著我的眼瞼。
風來了──彷若又回到當年，
一切還在──
淺山平原、紅蜻蜓、環頸雉⋯

還有水鳥，黃澄澄的稻浪──
都在我們面前。
是啊，一切都還在，
當我像匹小棕馬──只懂得馳騁
其間。
倘若還有下個世紀
或再等待個幾百年，
在這山海間，
是否還會有自然的光華，
或人與萬物共生的世界？
那兒──有山丘和草原，
還有迎面而來的野花和露水。
風來了──我聆聽──
沙沙的婆娑聲，──
秋蟬和蟲鳴⋯農家炊煙起
──妝點美麗的秋天。

Spruce Autumn Up　　　　　Lin Ming-Li

The ancient mountains and the sea line,
The ring of Formosa...
...Tilting my eyelids.
The wind comes — it is like to be back to those days,
Everything is still there —
Shallow mountain plains, red dragonflies, ring-necked pheasants...
As well as water birds, yellow waves of rice —
All before us.
Yeah, everything remains,
When I was like a little brown horse — who only knows galloping

In the meantime.
If there is still the next century
Or another few hundred years to wait,
In the mountain and sea,
Will there still be natural splendor,
Or a world of coexistence between man and all things?
There — there are hills and grasslands,
And the wild flowers and dew coming on.
The wind is coming — I listen —
The rustling, —
Autumn cicadas and insects…farm cooking smoke arising
— To spruce autumn up.

🍁 🍁 🍁

明朝 Ming Dynasty

83 •

於郡城送明卿之江西　　　　　　　李攀龍

青楓颯颯雨淒淒，秋色遙看入楚迷。
誰向孤舟憐逐客？白雲相送大江西。

Parting With a Banished Friend

Li Panlong

Green maple leaves are rustling
in the drizzling rain; the autumn

tints, from afar, are mistily dim
and distant. A banished official

in a lonely boat — who is going
to pity you? The white clouds

are sailing along with your sail,
until the west of the great river.

往事 林明理

即使不刻意
還尋
那小軒窗下
一彎白霧團團的溪

在此天涯海角
誰的舊夢裡
沒有偶爾
在青山間對著
那麼幾滴迷濛的雨

我願是那青煙
在你的呼喚中渺渺
側身而過。我願是露珠　戲跳蓮池
又回歸大地。

The Past Events Lin Ming-Li

Even if you do not deliberately
Look for
A bend of stream veiled in white mist
Under the window

In the ends of the earth
In whose old dreams
Occasionally
In the green mountains
Against a few drops of misty rain

I wish I were the smoke
Curling and floating by in your
Calling. I wish I were a dewdrop playing in the lotus pond
Before returning to the earth.

84 •

登泰山　　　　　　　　　　　　　　　　　　楊繼盛

志欲小天下，特來登泰山。
仰觀絕頂上，猶有白雲還。

Climbing Mount Tai　　　　　　Yang Jisheng

Cherishing an ambition
to overlook the world,

I come to climb and
conquer Mount Tai.

Atop the peak, up-
ward look — white

clouds are sailing at
ease, here and there.

元詩明理垂千載
古今抒情詩三百首
漢英對照

又見寒食 　　　　　　　　　　　林明理

雨添了許多聲浪
終將風吹在冰透的臉龐
而朝旭未露　泥路有馬車答答
從松嶺下來　迂迴繞過
是誰拂著樹葉漸漸被涼掃淨
投下更其烏黑的影
在遍地的濃溼中閃明

總是在想起妳的時候
急急地前進
妳聽，那春雷不經意地響了
四野的蛙鳴在淒切中開始
跟隨我依近竹籬外的青墳
我的愛
跨越千載　歸去
已是黃昏

Cold Food Day Again 　　　　Lin Ming-Li

The rain adds a lot of noises
Finally the wind blows in the face which is ice-cold
The morning sun is not revealed　the muddy road is splashing with horse carriages
Down from the pine ridge　roundabout
Who is blowing the leaves to be swept clean by the cool
Throw a shadow which is darker
Shining bright in the heavy wet everywhere

Thinking of you
Always rushing forward
Listen, the spring thunder is ringing by itself

Croaking of the wild frogs begins in a sad melody
Follow me to the green grave beyond the bamboo hedge
My love
Through thousands of years   returning
When it is dusk

🌿 🌿 🌿

85 •

山居夏日　　　　　　　　　　　　　　　　李江

綠滿柴扉日更長，天心徹底一方塘。
閑來獨向清風立，始覺荷花送遠香。

Mountain Living in Summer Days
　　　　　　　　　　　　　　　Li Jiang

The wooden gate is filled
with green when the day

is lengthening; the heart
of heaven is reflected in a

square pond. Idle, solitarily
I stand in the pure breeze,

and I sense the scent from
lotus blossoms wafting afar.

你從太陽裡走來

　　　　　　　　　　　　　　　　林明理

還記得嗎
溪谷裡芒花開了
又謝
你從太陽裡走來
讓每次春光都帶來幸福的圖彩
啊,曾經走過的
每一塊壘石每一方泥土
都沾滿你樸實的氣宇
你看,這長巷
曾無數次召喚著,而
你從不與黑暗同在
心似把火炬
照亮了山川錦綉
燃起了覺醒的光芒

啊,讓我飛吧,像雲那般
向著你離去的方向
那四季的足音
似乎馱來了新的訊息
一切都將過去的——
無數悲喜和泣別
都在風中沉沉地睡去了
就像夜空下
奮力滋長的葉瓣與蟲鳥
是那樣生機昂然,在
這碑林前,我輕輕地
輕輕地
為你獻上一束雅潔的
花香

You Come Out of the Sun   Lin Ming-Li

Do you still remember
Fern flowers are blossoming in the valley
And thank you
You come out of the sun
For each spring to bring happy colorful picture
Ah, each block of stone and each inch of soil
Ever walked over or through
Is tinctured with your simple air
You see, this long lane
Has called for countless times, and
You are never with the dark
The heart is like the torch
To light up the mountains and rivers
Enkindling the light of awakening

Oh, let me fly, like the clouds
In the direction of your departure
The footfall of the four seasons
Seems to carry a new message
All that are to pass away —
Countless joys and sorrows and tears
Have fallen asleep in the wind
Like in the night sky
The leaves growing vigorously, and birds & insects
Full of life, and
In front of the forest of tablets, gently I
Gently
Offer you a bouquet of
Fair flowers

元詩明理接千載
古今抒情詩三百首
漢英對照

86．

次韻和王文明絕句漫興十八首（其一）

劉基

芙蓉湖上夕陽低，楊柳枝頭一鳥棲。
獨倚闌幹看山色，白雲飛過若耶溪。

Eighteen Rambling Pieces (No. 1)　　Liu Ji

Over the lotus lake the
setting sun is hanging low;

atop the willow branch
a bird perches. Solitary

leaning against the balustrade
to admire the mountain,

when white clouds are
fleeting over a stream.

山茶

林明理

清秋
階沿邊的姿影
一瓣一葉的零落
被雨洗得白淨
一只蜻蜓貼近飛旋
閃著銀光的花朵

繞樹
去山畔默聽

流泉潺潺
人影雞聲
而我忘了秋雨
山茶
也立在風中

Camellia Flowers Lin Ming-Li

Pure autumn
The form along the steps
The petals and leaves are withering and falling
Washed white by the rain
A dragonfly flies close
To the silver shining flowers

Around the trees
Silent listening by the mountain
The babbling spring
Human forms and chicken crowing
And I have forgotten the autumn rain
The camellia flowers
Are also standing in the wind

夜泉 袁中道

山白鳥忽鳴，石冷霜欲結。
流泉得月光，化為一溪雪。

A Night Spring

Yuan Zhongdao

A white mountain,
a sudden bird

twitter; cold rocks,
frost to be frozen.

A running creek,
caught in the moon-

light, turns into
a creekful of snow.

在秋山的頂上守候

林明理

我從石井漬流
那綿亙的蓮花岩
如屏風守候
清波綠影
八月的陽光斑斕
妳的無邪
輕輕地開展山影顫動
炊煙升起
柿樹的黃葉零落
我在頂上等妳
等妳是澹白的一片霧光
我浮蕩的孤帆是單調的言語
發光的月
是我碎成幾塊的江心

Keeping Atop the Autumn Mountain
Lin Ming-Li

I flow from the stone well
The meandering lotus rocks
Keeping like a screen
Clear waves and green shadows
In August the brilliant sunshine
Your innocence
Gently spreading and the mountain shadow is trembling
Kitchen smoke arising
Persimmon tree leaves yellowing and flying
I wait for you atop the mountain
Waiting for you is a beam of pale white light
My floating solitary sail is monotonous speech
The luminous moon
Is the heart of the river which is broken into pieces

※ ※ ※

88 ·

次韻和王文明絕句漫興十八首（其五） 劉基

眼見繁花開滿林，即看嫩葉綠成陰。
杜鵑啼落西山月，一夜相思萬里心。

Eighteen Rambling Pieces (No. 5) Liu Ji

An eyeful of masses of flowering
blossoms filling the forest; tender

leaves are growing into heavy and
heavier shade. The cuckoo-bird twitters

until the moon over the western
mountain sets, when the nightlong

yearning means two hearts apart from
each other through thousands of miles.

懷舊 　　　　　　　　　　　　　　　林明理

往事是光陰的綠苔，
散雲是浮世的飄蓬。
雞鳴，我漫不經心地步移，
春歸使我愁更深。

一花芽開在我沉思之上，
孕蕾的幼蟲在悄然吐絲；
它細訴留痕的愛情，
縷縷如長夜永無開落。

Nostalgia 　　　　　　　　　　Lin Ming-Li

The past is the green moss of time,
Scattering clouds are the floating weeds of the world.
Chicken crowing, I carelessly move about,
Returning spring deepens my sorrow.

A flower bud blooms above my contemplation,
The larvas of the pregnant bud are quietly spinning silk;
It is telling the love of traces,
Continuously like a long night which never opens or closes.

89 ·

馬上作　　　　　　　　　　　　　　　戚繼光

南北驅馳報主情，江花邊月笑平生。
一年三百六十日，都是橫戈馬上行。

Composed on the Horseback　　Qi Jiguang

Galloping, to repay my
lord, hither and thither

to fight; riverside flowers
& border moon, all smiles,

witness my busy life. Three
hundred and sixty-five days

in a year, all are spent on
the back of the battle steed.

回憶的沙漏　　　　　　　　　　　　林明理

回憶的沙漏
滴滴滴下，似淚成河
我整夜輾轉反側
那小路上閃現的星光
是夏夜在那裡瞇著眼
從天幕的破處
傳來聲聲呼喚，縱橫錯落

大地上一切已從夢中醒覺
山影終將無法藏匿

我卻信，我將孤獨痛苦地
漫行於沙漠世界
夜，依然濃重
徜徉於
白堤的浮萍之間

The Hourglass of Memory Lin Ming-Li

The hourglass of memory
Drips and drops, like a river of tears
I toss and turn all night
The stars twinkling along the path
Are the summer night squinting
From the crack of the sky
The voices calling, crisscrossing

The earth has woken up from the dream
The mountain shadow eventually fails to hide up
And I believe, I will wander, lonely and
Painful, in the world of desert
The night, still heavy
Wandering
In the duckweed between the white banks

90．

五月十九日大雨 劉基

風驅急雨灑高城，雲壓輕雷殷地聲。
雨過不知龍去處，一池草色萬蛙鳴。

Caught in a Heavy Rain   Liu Ji

Driven by winds & rains, the
tall city is caught in a heavy

storm; clouds pressing thunders
low against the ground. Without

the foot of rain, without the
trace of the rain-dragon —

a grassy pool is noisy with
myriads of croaking frogs.

雨落在故鄉的泥土上   林明理

一、
雨落在故鄉的泥土上
你看見了嗎
沒有人可遺忘
奧斯威辛集中營
終於，那些殺人魔被聖火吞噬
終於，那不屈的靈魂
得以解脫

告訴我，親愛的
為什麼我的手心裡
還殘存著你的溫柔
為什麼風像個無家可歸的老婦
徘徊在這廣場
而你
已遺忘了槍尖上的哀嚎

二、
雨落在故鄉的泥土上
你看見了嗎
那白色魔窟
是製造殺人病毒的工廠
他們把病毒灑向世界
在掠奪，在刑求
還無情地發出狂笑

啊告訴我，親愛的
為什麼我的胸口
會有撕裂般的痛
為什麼雨像個情人
徘徊在這原野裡
而你
已沉睡在石碑下

三、
雨落在故鄉的泥土上
你看見了嗎
沒有人可遺忘
紀念碑裡的故事
當我閉上眼
就能朗讀你的笑容
就像五千年前的太陽
那麼燦亮

啊告訴我，親愛的
為什麼我的喉管裡
流淌著你的淚水

為什麼雨像個浪子
狂飆在這林道
而你
已然像個雕像　不再憂愁

The Raindrops Are Falling in My Hometown
          Lin Ming-Li

1.
The raindrops are falling in my hometown
Do you see it
Nobody can be forgotten
The Auschwitz Concentration Camp
Finally, those devil killers were devoured by the holy flames
Finally, the unyielding souls
Were set free

Tell me, dear
Why is your tenderness
Is still warm in my hands
Why is the wind loitering in the square
Like a homeless old woman
And you
Have forgotten the screams at gunpoint

2.
The raindrops are falling in my hometown
Do you see it?
The white den of monsters
Is a factory manufacturing poison to kill people
They spread poison all over the world
Looting, torturing,
And laughing mercilessly

Oh please tell me, dear
Why is there such a ripping pain
In my chest
Why is the rain lingering about the field
Like a lover
And you
Are sound asleep under the stone tablet

3.
The raindrops are falling in my hometown
Do you see it?
Nobody can be forgotten
The story in the monument
When I close my eyes
I can read your smiling face
As bright as the sun
Of five thousand years ago

Oh please tell me, dear
Why your tears are flowing
In my throat?
Why is the rain running wild like a vagabond
Along the woods path
And you
Like a statue　sorrowful no more

91·

題沙溪驛　　　　　　　　　　　　　　劉基

澗水彎彎繞郡城，老蟬嘶作車輪聲。
西風吹客上馬去，夕陽滿川紅葉明。

The Station of Sand & Stream   Liu Ji

The creek river meanders along
about the town; the cicadas, old

now, are chirping like the creaking
voice of rumbling wheels. Blown

in the west wind, the wanderer
mounts the horse, when all rivers

are filled with the setting sun, and all
the crimson leaves are dancing brilliant.

永安鹽田濕地   林明理

一條碎石小路
黃昏的堤岸
　　無人走過
三五白鷺
　　低低地
飛往泥灘

寂寞的鹽田啊
　　更遠處
還有高高
踮起腳尖的水鳥
夜鷺在風中
　　嘎嘎啼叫

是的，這一帶
曾是候鳥的天堂

而我所企盼的
　　恰如這清風
　　從紅樹林傳來的
　　鳥聲越來越近
　　　月在水上

The Yongan Wetland[32] 　　　Lin Ming-Li

　A gravel path
　The bank at dusk
Nobody passing by
　Except a few egrets
Flying low
　Towards the mud beach

　　The lonely salty field
Oh farther away
　And the tall
　　Waterfowls standing on their tiptoes
　　The night herons in the wind
Are howling

　　Yes, this area
　　Used to be the paradise for migratory birds
　　What I expect now
Is just like the breeze
　　Traveling from the mangroves
　　The twitters of birds are close and closer
The moon is on the water

---

[32] the Yongan Wetland in Kaohsiung has ever been the largest salty flat wetland south of Tainan, with a history of salt culture, mangrove ecology and valuable migratory bird resources.

92·

春蠶　　　　　　　　　　　　　　　　劉基

可笑春蠶獨苦辛，為誰成繭卻焚身。
不如無用蜘蛛網，網盡蜚蟲不畏人。

Spring Silkworm　　　　　　　　　Liu Ji

Laughable: the spring silkworm spares no efforts —

for whom do you toil and
moil? To be cocooned, to

be imprisoned! The spider
web is useless: yet it catches

all the flying insects and
worms, unafraid of humans.

水蓮　　　　　　　　　　　　　　　　林明理

以簡
而婉約
歌頌，在水一方
又回到沉思的外貌

而陽光
用心地點描

只有一經晨露了,才在
瞻仰的青空裡跟著
喜悅和凝望

而漂泊的我
也感悟自己的微小

Water Lilies　　　　　　　　　Lin Ming-Li

With simple
And graceful
Praise, beyond the water
And back to the appearance of contemplation

And the sunshine
Attentively describes

It is only after the morning dew
That I follow joy and gaze
In the sky of contemplation

Adrift I
Also feel my smallness

93·

天平山中　　　　　　　　　　　　楊基

細雨茸茸濕楝花,南風樹樹熟枇杷。
徐行不記山深淺,一路鶯啼送到家。

In the Heaven-Flat Mountain   Yang Ji

A fine rain, drizzling and drozzling,
moistens chinaberry flowers;

the southernly wind blows to
ripen a treeful after another treeful

of loquats. Slow strolling in the
mountain now deep and then

shallow; orioles are twittering all
the way — homeward, until home.

坐覺   林明理

我的坐覺是　在俯仰間
如何稟持一種
如水月般的自若

在微雨瀟瀟的夜裡
如何能輕輕想起
那寺院的鐘
破曉的雲和那些葉落
鏗然的聲音
在寒意深重的此刻
如何能在多情的明燈前
默默不語的伴我讀書　對坐
而山雨　悄悄地停了

憶往之夢　也真的不再頻頻回首

我的坐覺是　昨日之後
如何讓明天更懂得以一種
無有罣礙的心情　隨緣
喜捨

Sitting Sensation　　　　　　　　Lin Ming-Li

My sitting sensation is　between looking up and down
How to hold a kind of calm
Like the moon in water

In the night of drizzling rain
How to gently think
Of the temple bell
The dawn clouds and those falling leaves
The sonorous voice
At the moment of chilliness
Before the passionate bright lamp
To silently accompany me reading　sitting together
The mountain rain　has quietly stopped

The dream of past memories　really without frequent looking back

My sitting sensation is　after yesterday
How for tomorrow to know better
In a free mood　as it is fated
Joyful giving

94 ·

玉蘭　　　　　　　　　　　　　　　睦石

霓裳片片晚妝新，束素亭亭玉殿春。
已向丹霞生淺暈，故將清露作芳塵。

Magnolia Flowers　　　　　　　Sui Shi

Neon-like clothes, a piece
after another piece, all new

evening dresses; a bouquet after
another bouquet of white flowers

against the pavilions & temples
in spring. Towards the rosy dawn,

light pink is born; the pure dew
drops into the scented earth.

魯花樹[33]　　　　　　　　　　　　林明理

一棵百歲魯花樹
　　蓬勃地長著
金晃晃的葉縫間
那闇影，多麼安靜
　　使人愉悅

鮮麗的漿果
由綠　而黃　而紅

---

[33] 魯花樹據說是花東地區原住民語的音譯，原住民取其樹幹為搗小米用的杵，排灣族以其根莖做黑褐色的染料。

織就了無數個童年
而我視線之下
天頂的白雲冉冉翻飛

每當風神前來糾纏
枝上歌雀齊鳴
它便伸長脖頸
將往來的面孔或光陰的
故事，都一一收藏

The Tree of Scolopia Oldhamii[34]

Lin Ming-Li

A tree of scolopia oldhamii of one hundred years
    Is growing and flourishing
Amid the golden leaves
The shadows, how quiet
    And pleasant

The fresh berries
    From green to yellow and to red
Weaving countless childhoods
    And beneath my eyes
The white clouds overhead are flying freely

Each time the wind god comes to pester
    The songbirds on the branches sing together
And it stretches its neck
To collect the faces to and fro
As well as the stories of time

---

[34] The tree of scolopia oldhamii is said to be the transliteration of the indigenous language of Huadong Area; the indigenous people take its trunk as a pestle for millet, and the Paiwan people use its roots to make black brown dye.

95·

奇跡武塘賦之 夏完淳

逢花卻憶故園梅,雪掩寒山徑不開。
明月愁心兩相似,一枝素影待人來。

Lodging in Wutang Xia Wanchun

The sight of flowers in Wutang
reminds me of native plum

blossoms; covered with a blanket
of snow, all the paths in the cold

mountain are blocked. The bright
moon shares the sorrow in my

heart, when a twig of fair form
is waiting for my return from afar.

你的呼喚—to 普希金[35] Aleksandr Pushkin（1799-1837） 林明理

你的呼喚
能夠引起千萬個親切的懷念
眾神圍繞著你的步履

---

[35] 普希金鎮 沙皇村（Царское село）。

繁星垂掛在你的胸前
雪花輕輕唱
莫札特樂曲隱隱約約
我讀皇村的花園
紅梅花兒正開
如讀你不朽的詩篇

Your Calling — To Aleksandr Pushkin[36]（1799-1837） Lin Ming-Li

Your calling
Can evoke a thousand fond remembrances
All gods go about your steps
The maze of stars hang on your chest
Snowflakes are singing gently
The music of Mozart is soft and faint
I read the garden of the Royal Village
The red plum blossoms are flowering
Like reading your immortal poems

🍀 🍀 🍀

96 ·

題葡萄圖　　　　　　　　　　徐渭

半生落魄已成翁，獨立書齋嘯晚風。
筆底明珠無處賣，閑拋閑擲野藤中。

---

[36] the Royal Village of Pushkin Town.

Inscription on a Painting of Grapes
                                         Xu Wei

Down and out for half a lifetime, I am
an old man now. Alone in my lone study,

I face the evening breeze. A draggy sale:
heaps of black-pearl-like grapes, so rich

and fine, are found all spread about, trod
to pieces, some here, some there, as

harvest from beneath my brush, in and
into, the tangled mass of wild vegetation.

眼睛深處   林明理

初冬的晨霧盤踞山頭
溪上煙波浩渺
那曾經的愛情
無遠弗屆，不分時空

一隻斑文鳥
躺在芒草叢的光裡
眨著眼睛說：傻瓜，真愛無疆
應及時把握

Deep in the Eye   Lin Ming-Li

The morning mist in early winter is spreading over the mountain
The stream is misty with boundless waves
The love that has ever been
No distance, regardless of time & space

A bird of lonchura punctulata
Is lying in the light of the Chinese silvergrass
Winking its eyes to say: dear, true love has no boundary
Which should be cherished in time

97 ·

龕山凱歌　　　　　　　　　　　　徐渭

短劍隨槍暮合圍，寒風吹血著人飛。
朝來道上看歸騎，一片紅冰冷鐵衣。

A Triumphant Song in Kanshan Mountain
Xu Wei

Flashing swords and gleaming
spears, encirclement of the

dusk; chilly wind blowing
blood, clinging to human

clothes. Early morning finds
cavaliers returning along

the way — a mass of red
ice & cold clothes of iron.

佛羅里達山獅[37]

林明理

沿著河流拐彎處
除了風,月光,草蟲聲
　一切靜寂
牠緩慢而謹慎地
　　望向一台隱藏攝影機
然後,踮起腳尖
　　　迅速逃離而去
這掠食者,被監視——
　恐懼於草木之中

Dr. Mingli Lin painting work in Taiwan／Florida Panther
佛羅里達山獅／林明理 2017 年畫作

Florida Panther[38]

Lin Ming-Li

Along the bend of the river
Except for winds, insect chirping, the moonshine
　Quietness reigns everywhere
Slowly and cautiously
　It looks at the hidden video camera
Then, on tiptoe
　　Flees in a hurry
The predator, when overseen —
　Is startled into grass & woods

---

[37] 佛羅里達山獅 Florida Panther(學名:*Puma concolor coryi*),又名美洲獅,牠們現存的數量估計僅為 100 多隻。有生態學家認為,科學家的監視器可能對這些掠食者造成恐懼,促使牠們花更多的時間在逃跑的狀態,因此影響進食時間也比較少。值得關注。

[38] Florida Panther (scientific name: Puma concolor coryi), also named puma, with estimated small number of only over 100. It is believed by some ecologists that the video camera set by the scientists may bring horror to these predators and drive them running about for life, thus influencing their diet. Attention should be paid to this.

98.

風鳶圖詩 　　　　　　　　　　　　徐渭

柳條搓線絮搓棉，搓夠千尋放紙鳶。
消得春風多少力，帶將兒輩上青天。

Flying the Kite 　　　　　　　　　Xu Wei

Willowy twigs as the line,
catkin as the cotton; rolling

and twisting, when adequately
long, to fly the kite. How much

spring wind, how many efforts
are made to fly up the kite —

heavenward; hopefully, children
can make progress likewise.

巴巴里獅[39] 　　　　　　　　　　　林明理

曾經奔馳數千年
像個草原霸主

---

[39] 巴巴里獅（Panthera leo leo），是世界上最大隻的獅子，也叫北非獅 barbary lion，以往分布在北非，由摩洛哥至埃及，但1922年後最後一隻野外的巴巴里獅被射殺後，在非洲北部生存了幾千年的巴巴里獅終於在北非銷聲匿跡。現在可能只有低於40隻飼養的巴巴里獅，在動物園或馬戲園內可看見。還有，在英國倫敦的特拉法加廣場納爾遜紀念碑的獅子雕塑原型，就是巴巴里獅，也格外有雄武的風度。

牠有清澈的灰色眼睛
　白沙似的皮膚和
　濃密的黑鬃　流蘇般
遮住了腹部⋯
如今，牠小憩在
納爾遜紀念碑前
安靜無聲，彷彿已然消逝

Dr. Mingli Lin painting work in Taiwan Panthera leo leo
巴巴里獅／2017 年 8 月林明理畫作

Panthera Leo Leo[40]　　　　　Lin Ming-Li

　For thousands of years
　It has been the master of the grassland
　With its clear gray eyes
White sandy skin
And thick black mane
　Covering its abdomen ...
Now it is resting quietly
　At the foot of Nelson Monument
　As if it has already disappeared

---

[40] Panthera leo leo is the largest lion in the world, also known as the North African lion barbary lion, used to be distributed in North Africa, from Morocco to Egypt, but after 1922, the last wild Barbary lion was shot, in northern Africa for thousands of years, and the Barbary lion finally disappeared in North Africa. Today there are probably fewer than 40 Barbary lions in captivity, seen in zoos or circuses. In addition, the lion sculpture prototype of Nelson's Monument in Trafalgar Square in London, England, is the Barbary lion, which is particularly with a heroic air.

99·

王元章倒枝梅畫　　　　　　　　　　徐渭

皓態孤芳壓俗姿，不堪複寫拂雲枝。
從來萬事嫌高格，莫怪梅花著地垂。

A Painting of Sprawling Plum Flowers　　Xu Wei

White form and solitary
scent, detached from all

vulgar forms; clouds-
scraping branches are hard

to be painted. Myriads of
things hate to be high-profiled;

no wonder: plum blossoms are
blossoming against the ground.

大雪山[41]風景　　　　　　　　　　林明理

當夕陽將盡
　層層雲海
從淡紫變成緋紅
　飄滿天際。
一隻松鴉飛起，
　點亮村舍的燈火。

---

[41] 大雪山位於台灣苗栗縣泰安鄉與台中市和平區交界處，為台灣的名山。

在大雪山
　　林海的初冬之中，
　我夢見了冬螢飛舞，
　　飛鼠鳴唱。
風和月兒攜手散步，
山羌豎起耳朵——
　　傾聽我的詩思。
夜是朦朧的，
星際的樹梢⋯
　　⋯越黑越閃亮。
思念無邊，恰如
部落的歌聲　緩緩
　　流瀉而來。

The Scenery of the Daxue Mountain[42]

Lin Ming-Li

When the setting sun sets
Layers of clouds as a sea
From pale purple to crimson
Floating in the sky.
A jay is flying,
To enkindle the lamps in the cottage.
In the Daxue Mountain
In the early winter of the sea of trees,
I dream of the fireflies flying in winter,
And the flying rats singing.
The wind and the moon walk together,

---

[42] Daxue Mountain, a famous mountain in Taiwan, is located at the junction of Tai'an Township, Miaoli County, and Heping District, Taichung City.

Hawthorns raise their ears —
To listen to my poems.
The night is dim and hazy,
Interstellar treetops...
...The darker the more shiny.
The boundless longing, like
The song of the tribe, slowly
Flowing towards me.

100 ·

天河　　　　　　　　　　　　徐渭

天河下看匡瀑垂，桑蛾蠶口一絲飛。
昨宵殺虱三十個，亦報將軍破月支。

The Heavenly River　　　　　Xu Wei

Looking down from the heavenly
river, a waterfall is hanging in

the mid-air; mulberry ears and
silkworm mouths are like flying

threads. Last night thirty lice have
been killed, which is reported as

military exploits: the enemy border
has been crossed and conquered.

在北極荒野中　　　　　　　　　　林明理

一個科學家停下腳步，
看著懸崖下的永凍土層
被地球暖化後…慢慢
滑入大海
感到自己是如此孤獨。

不由得坐在沼澤旁，
信手拾得隨風飄散
毛茸茸的莢果，
想起長滿羊鬍子草的原野
和遊隼歌唱的天空

那遍野的洋甘菊
如此熟悉
麝牛還在島嶼邊緣吃草
棲息地底的旅鼠
仍探頭瞅瞅著

一個因紐特老人說，
「我只希望下一代，
再下一代能看到白鯨
和魚群，在我們咫尺之外
別無他求。」

科學家自嘲地笑笑。
誰也不知在時間軸中
最後定格於何時？
在北極荒野
與世界的疼痛之後

In the Arctic Wilderness   Lin Ming-Li

A scientist stops and
Watches the permafrost beneath the cliff
warms up by the earth....slowly
Sliding into the sea
And I feel alone.

I could not help sitting by the marsh
Picking up fluffy pods
To be scattered in the wind
Thinking of the fields covered with sheepbeard grass
And the sky aloud with the singing of peregrine falcons

Chamomiles fill the field
So familiar
The muskoxen are grazing on the edge of the island
The lemmings at the bottom of the habitat
Are tentatively looking and peering

An old Inuit says
I hope the next generation
And the generation which follows, can see beluga whales
And schools of fish, a few feet away from us
And nothing more

The scientist laughs mockingly
Nobody knows in the timeline
What time is set
In the Arctic wilderness
After the pain of the world

101・

葡萄 徐渭

璞中美玉石般看，畫裡名珠煞欲穿。
世事模糊多少在，付之一笑向青天。

Grapes Xu Wei

A gem out of a rough
diamond, to be taken

as a tone; a painting of
paintings, without a parallel.

How many events have
become dim and distant

— all laughed away —
heavenward laughing.

你的榮光[43]——給 prof. Ernesto Kahan
林明理

我敬佩你，朋友，
和平的使者
　悲憫的心胸。
聖潔的目光
比藍天還清澄，
深深浸潤著學子心田，

---

[43] 這是 2018 年 11 月的印度獎，該獎項是印度兩所大學的榮譽博士，以表彰 prof. Ernesto Kahan 對全球和平、愛與和諧的奉獻精神。

也不可分地貫穿在
愛與和諧之中。

Photo: Ernesto Kahan won the award

Your Glory— To Professor Ernesto Kahan[44]

Lin Ming-Li

I admire you, dear friend
The messenger of peace
With a compassionate heart
Your holy eyes
Are more limpid than the blue sky
Penetrating the hearts of the students
And through
Love and harmony

✤ ✤ ✤

102 ·

石灰吟　　　　　　　　　　　　　　　　　　于謙

千錘萬鑿出深山，烈火焚燒若等閒。
粉骨碎身渾不怕，要留清白在人間。

---

[44] Professor Ernesto Kahan was awarded, in November, 2018, an honorable doctorate degree by two universities in India for his dedication.

The Limestone   Yu Qian

Cutting, carving, chiseling
— out of the deep mountain;

burning, searing, scorching
— it counts for nothing.

Broken to pieces, or even
powdered — nothing to

dread, so long as purity,
in the world, remains.

信天翁[45]   林明理

我是逆風飛翔的歌者
不管殺人鯨或雪鳥
　　呼嘯而過
我還是我
總離不開海上或島嶼
離不開
淨白無缺的天空

Lin Mingli/painting

生命有時需要一點運氣
或冒險才得以生存
但生存何其不易
一切可能不如預期
或者邪惡總在

---

[45] 大多數的信天翁生活在南半球深海區域的範圍內。人們通常在大洋航行時，在海上或石礁島嶼等地方可看到信天翁。牠是世界上翅膀最長的鳥類。

黑暗中流動
但我的歌──

有著愉悅的喧噪
不管你信不信
　　我還是我
我喜歡獨立的思想家
他們能盡情地想像
而想像恰如我漫漫旅程中
　　一首純真的歌

The Albatross[46]   Lin Ming-Li

I am a singer flying against the wind
No matter whales or snowbirds
Whistling by
I am still me
I cannot do without the sea or islands
Cannot be away
From the pure white sky

Occasionally life needs a bit of luck
And adventure to survive
But survival is no easy matter
Not everything is as expected
Evil is constantly
Moving in darkness
But my songs —

---

[46] Most albatross live in the deep-sea region of the southern hemisphere, and they are often seen on islands such as the Isle of Rocks, during ocean voyage. The birds have the longest wings in the world.

With pleasant noises
Believe it or not
I am still me
I like independent thinkers
Who indulge in their imagination
Which is like a pure song
In my long journey

※ ※ ※

103.

除夜太原寒甚　　　　　　　　　于謙

寄語天涯客，輕寒底用愁。
春風來不遠，只在屋東頭。

The Cold New Year's Eve in Taiyuan
Yu Qian

Please tell the wanderer
in the horizon: no worry

about the slight cold —
spring wind is around

the corner — not far from
the east end of the house.

夢見中國　　　　　　　　　　　林明理

在極美的十月裡
我以真摯之眼凝望你

水一樣澄澈，火一樣灼熱
聽，海濤聲那樣悠揚
我一腳在臺灣，一腳在中國
就這樣忘卻了一切苦痛
我努力睜大了眼，望向聲音來源
你的影子
以及無數勤奮的身姿——
宛如一大片金沙
圍繞著我舞蹈

我是真的來過這兒
或只是錯覺？
是夢，又不是夢
歲月如流，你露出光潔的面容
彷彿碩大的寶石
我願是海邊的一個水手
依附著一大片溫暖的黑暗
然後，我聽見了浪潮聲
也聞到海草的味道
是你
招來璀璨的朝陽
將我擁抱

Dreaming of China

Lin Ming-Li

In the most beautiful October
I look at you with sincere eyes
As limpid as water, as hot as fire
Listen, it is melodious as the sound of the sea
One foot in Taiwan and one foot in China
Thus I forget all the pains

I try to open my eyes wide, looking at the source of voice
Your shadow
And countless diligent forms —
Like a large stretch of gold sand
Dancing around me

Have I really been here
Or it is a mere illusion?
A dream, and not a dream
The years go like running water, you show a brilliant face
Like a great jewel
I wish I were a sailor on the seashore
Clinging to a large stretch of warm darkness
Then I hear the sea waves
And smell the seaweed
It is you
Who bring the bright morning sun
To embrace me

104·

上太行山 于謙

西風落日草斑斑，雲薄秋空鳥獨還。
兩鬢霜華千里客，馬蹄又上太行山。

Climbing the Taihang Mountain Yu Qian

The setting sun shines over withered
grass blown in the west wind; through

thin clouds wafting in the autumnal sky
a bird returns by itself. Frosty-templed,

a wanderer is thousands of miles away
from his home, when the clip-clop of

his horse brings the rider upward —
upward in the Taihang Mountain.

它的名字叫山陀兒[47]   林明理

在福爾摩沙
萬物
異常的靜。

混沌夜影中
只有他在施暗計
一邊隱伏，一邊飛旋

貫穿於濕透的大地
有如一隻脫了韁
滿眼赭紅的大怪獸。

Its Name is Shantar[48]   Lin Ming-Li

In Formosa
Everything
Is unusually quiet.

---

[47] 中度颱風山陀兒（國際命名為「KRATHON」），於二〇二四年十月三日侵襲臺灣後，造成重大傷害，因而為詩。

[48] Moderate Typhoon Santar, internationally named "KRATHON", has caused significant damage after hitting Taiwan on October 3, 2024, hence the poem.

In the dark shadows of the night
Only he is scheming
Lurking, and spinning

Running through the sodden earth
Like a monster with loose
Rein and red eyes.

                                              一 October 3, 2024.

105 ·

絕筆　　　　　　　　　　　　　　　　　　唐寅

一日兼他兩日狂，已過三萬六千場。
他年新識如相問，只當飄流在異鄉。

The Last Words　　　　　　　　　Tang Yin

One day is lived and spent as
two days — thirty-six thousand

days in the lifetime, all in all.
This world and the nether world

一 no substantial difference.
In case some new acquaintance

asks about me, tell him: I am
wandering in a foreign land.

元詩明理邁千載
古今抒情詩三百首
漢英對照

如風往事　　　　　　　　　　林明理

終究
一切都已結束
終究
讓愛遠颺
終究
獨自步上荊棘之路
我的靈魂懸在崖壁
　　邊游邊躲

是誰
讓一切返回虛無
是誰
兀自矗立懸崖之後
不再夢寐以求什麼
愛，可以反覆難測
也可以歸於平淡……
　　來去無蹤

Gone With the Wind　　　Lin Ming-Li

Eventually
Everything is over
Eventually
For love to fly away
Eventually
Alone on a thorny road
My soul is hanging over the cliff
　　Wandering and hiding

Who is it
Making everything return to nothingness

Who is it
After climbing the cliff
Dreaming no more of anything
Love, which can be unfathomable
And can be insignificant…
   Coming and going without any trace

🌳 🌳 🌳

106·

奉寄孫思和   唐寅

領解皇都第一名，猖披歸臥舊茅蘅。
立錐莫笑無餘地，萬里江山筆下生。

To My Friend Sun Sihe   Tang Yin

Unique and number one in
understanding the imperial capital,

I retreat to reside in an old thatched
cottage as a bohemian. No laugh:

in spite of a tiny bit of room,
thousands of miles of hills & rills

are represented, vividly and
spectacularly, under my brush.

致珍古德博士（Dr. Jane Goodall）   林明理

妳，聖美與愛的天使
深入高山田野，為黑猩猩請命

為保育而日以繼夜
而所有榮光已種在地球村的
每一角落，化成一首真理的詩

To Dr. Jane Goodall Lin Ming-Li

You, angel of love and holy beauty
Deep into fields and high mountains, pleading for the chimpanzees
Work day and night for conservation
And all the glory has been planted in each corner
Of the global village, turning into a poem of truth

🌿 🌿 🌿

107 ·

壽王少傅守溪 唐寅

綠蓑煙雨江南客，白髮文章閣下臣。
同在太平天子世，一雙空手掌絲綸。

Keeping and Watching the Creek
Tang Yin

Green palm-bark rain cape,
a wanderer in the Southern

Shore veiled in mist & rain;
white hair and articles as a

minister in the imperial palace.
In the piping times of peace,

the empty hands holding
nothing but a fishing rod.

平靜的湖面 　　　　　　　　　　　　　林明理

在淡淡白色煙霧裡
你是思索中的詩人
看落葉褪盡
季節輪換的容貌

The Calm Lake 　　　　　　　　　Lin Ming-Li

In the dim white fog
You are a poet lost in deep thought
Watching the leaves fading and falling
And the changing visage of the season

🌿 🌿 🌿

108．

言志 　　　　　　　　　　　　　　　唐寅

不煉金丹不坐禪，不為商賈不耕田。
閑來寫就青山賣，不使人間造孽錢。

My Ambition 　　　　　　　　　　Tang Yin

Neither alchemy nor
religious meditations;

neither business nor tilling
field. When idle, I paint

元詩明理堪千載
古今抒情詩三百首
漢英對照

some paintings of fair
hills & rills which are sold

for money, instead of ill-
gotten money or filthy lucre.

路 　　　　　　　　　　　　　　　　　林明理

一條無盡的路
橫臥在巨峰之間。
僅少數的村人，僧侶
沿著這路蜿蜒向前⋯

擁抱世界的夢想，
從青春的少年
到孤獨的暮年，
生命轉瞬即逝；

蒼天許我以歌——
像隻黑頭文鳥
在田野中自由飛翔，
領受大地賜給我的恩典。

The Road 　　　　　　　　　　Lin Ming-Li

An endless road
Lies between the peaks of the mountain
Only a few villagers and monks
Go on along this road...

The dream to embrace the world
From the time of youth

To the lonely old age
Life is in an instant

Heaven gives me a song —
Like a blackbird
I fly freely in the field
To receive the grace the earth bestows upon me

🍀 🍀 🍀

109 ·

口號三首（其一）   祝允明

枝山老子鬢蒼浪，萬事遺來剩得狂。
從此日和先友對，十年漢晉十年唐。

Three Impromptu Poems (No. 1)
Zhu Yunming

An old man now, I am gray-
templed; myriads of past events

are forgotten, except for my
arrogance. Hence I make friends

with the ancients through reading
day after day: ten years steeped

in Han and Jin dynasties and
another ten years, in Tang dynasty.

元詩明理耀千載
古今抒情詩三百首
漢英對照

父親的手　　　　　　　　　　　　　　　林明理

打開記憶之門
牽著父親的手
在安靜的小路上…
一步一步
向今天
走來

Father's Hands　　　　　　　　　　　Lin Ming-Li

Open the door of memory
Holding Father's hands
Along the quiet road….
A step after a step
Walking toward
Today

❋ ❋ ❋

110·

夏口夜泊別友人　　　　　　　　　　　李夢陽

黃鶴樓前日欲低，漢陽城樹亂烏啼。
孤舟夜泊東遊客，恨殺長江不向西。

Parting With a Friend　　　　　　　Zhu Yunming

Before the Yellow Crane Tower,
the sun hangs low; in the opposite

Hanyang town, the trees are noisy
with cawing crows. A lonely boat

is tethered for night lodging of the
east-bound wanderer — the Yangtze

River, like it or not, keeps running
eastward, instead of westward...

我將獨行 　　　　　　　　　　　　林明理

多少次
我們走過這小徑，
月寂寂。山脈諦聽著海音
夜鷺緩踱

大海看似平靜
肥沃的田野睡在星輝中
總是相視、無語
細碎的足聲踏響整個天際

今日，我將獨行——
依然走在這條舊路
你已遠去，而我心悠悠
重逢是未來歲月的憂愁

I Will Walk Alone 　　　　　　Lin Ming-Li

How many times
We have walked along the path
Silent is the moon. The mountains are listening to the sound
of the sea
The night heron is slowly pacing

The sea seems to be calm
The fertile field is asleep in the starlight
Always looking at each other, wordless
The sound of footsteps is echoing across the sky

Today, I will walk alone —
Still along the old path
You are far away, and my heart is pensive
Reunion is the sorrow of the future years

🌳 🌳 🌳

111·

汴中元夕五首（其一）　　　　　李夢陽

花燭沉沉動玉樓，月明春女大堤遊。
空中騎吹名王過，散落天聲滿汴州。

Five Poems About the Lantern Festival in Kaifeng (No. 1)　　Li Mengyang

Flowery candles upon candles
are flickering in the towers of

jade; young girls, bathed in the
bright moonlight, are sauntering

and strolling along the banks.
Riding while blowing and piping

in mid-air, clustering round the
king — heavenly voices are

wafting, scattering and falling,
filling the whole city of Kaifeng.

Love Is... 林明理

Love is
交會的眼神
　驚喜的一瞬
沒有虛飾
　彷若重生
沒有謊言
　只有真誠
它是自由的風
　不羈而難覓
哪怕是寸步千里
或千山萬水
無須承諾
沒有怨尤
Love is near you
在心的最深處

Love Is.... Lin Ming-Li

Love is
The moment of pleasant surprise
When the eyes meet
Without pretention
Like a rebirth
Without lies
Only sincerity
It is the free wind
Carefree and hard to find

Either small steps and thousands of miles
Or thousands of hills and rills
No need of promises
No complaints
Love is near you
From the bottom of heart

112 ·

汴中元夕五首（其二） 　　　李夢陽

玉館朱城柳陌斜，宋京燈月散煙花。
門外香車若流水，不知青鳥向誰家。

Five Poems About the Lantern Festival in Kaifeng (No. 2) — Li Mengyang

Sumptuous houses in the red town where
willows are waving aslant; in the capital

of the Song dynasty, the lamps, lanterns,
and the moon are watching the explosion

of fireworks. Beyond the gate, graceful
and colorful carriages are running like

running water — the blue bird, who
knows, flies to alight in which house?

北風

經了萬年雪
再遠的路
也會奮起攀過
彼岸遙望

輕雲在山口等候
故鄉的面孔愈來愈清
在無止盡的漂泊裡
眼睛，偶爾也會隱隱，作痛

一顆孤星仍在亭臺
在茱萸依然盈手的階下
閃著如朝露般的未來

The North Wind   Lin Mingli

Through ten thousand years of snow
In spite of the distance of the road
It will be covered with efforts
Looking at the opposite shore

Light clouds are waiting in the mountain pass
The visage of hometown is more and more clear
In the endless wandering
Occasionally the eyes are faintly painful

A lone star is still standing in the pavilion
Under the steps where the dogwood still fills the hands
Flashing with a future like the morning dew

元詩明理搖千載
古今詩情詩三百首
漢英對照

113．

汴中元夕五首（其三）   李夢陽

中山孺子倚新妝，鄭女燕姬獨擅場。
齊唱憲王春樂府，金梁橋外月如霜。

Five Poems About the Lantern Festival in Kaifeng (No. 3)   Li Mengyang

Youths from the Central Plain are
gaudy in their costumes, and young

girls of the northern lands are consummate
as artists. They come from various

places to Kaifeng, to sing the songs
and giving the performances by King

Xian of Zhou — the voices and noises
continue from day to night, until the

moon comes out, to be brilliant, casting
a coat of frost upon the Golden Bridge.

愛的箴言   林明理

如果有人問
當愛情回到我身邊
噢，該如何想像——
又有誰說得清或膽敢說出
它真摯的美

它是一種魔藥
無法加以防備
如果愛情回到我身邊…
…它不是用來及時行樂
或瞻仰在虛空的晨星

而虛空的晨星──俱已消逝
卻總會又不經意地重現
它純粹是一種感覺
是世間無可比擬…
…亙古不墜的神話

當愛情回到我身邊
噢,我會記起你的微笑
它流過秋天的楓香小徑
從躲藏其間的風
到窺伺的星星

The Proverb of Love   Lin Mingli

If somebody asks
When love comes back to me
Oh, how to imagine it —
Who can make it clear or dare to tell
Its sincere beauty

It is like a potion
Which cannot be guarded against
If love comes back to me....
…It is not to enjoy it while one can
Or to admire the morning stars in the void

And the morning stars in the void — all are gone
But they will reappear inadvertently
It is purely a kind of feeling
It is unparalleled in the world....
…The myth of immortality

When love comes back to me
Oh I will remember your smile
It flows along the autumnal path scented with maple leaves
From the wind hiding in it
To the peeping stars

114 ·

汴中元夕五首（其四）　　　　李夢陽

四海煙花逢上元，中州行樂競千門。
大江不辨魚龍戲，珊瑚寶玦是王孫

Five Poems About the Lantern Festival in Kaifeng (No. 4)　　Li Mengyang

Fireworks from the four seas
converge here at the Lantern Festival,

when the Central State is joyous
and festive from door to door. Over

the great river, no distinction of
the play of fish and dragon, corals

and penannular jade rings are
worn by the prince's descendants.

寫給包公故里──肥東　　　　　　林明理

是怎樣的企盼，怎樣的憧憬？
讓我飛越海洋的邊界，泊在巢湖之畔，
等待無比明顯的希望之城──肥東。

是的，你就像心中的巨人，堅毅而平和。
輕快的白雲，群山和寧靜的沃土
都在我的血液中搏動。
溪流在岩邊跳著舞，古民也唱出心中的歌。

今夜，我依舊做著旅人的夢，
夢裡用眼睛尾隨著飛逝的船隻，
我感到莫名的幸福。

To Bao Gong's Hometown — Feidong

Lin Ming-Li

What kind of hope, what kind of longing?
Let me fly across the boundary of the ocean, to moor on the side of Chaohu Lake
To wait for the incomparably obvious city of hope — Feidong.

Yes, you are like a giant in the heart, firm and peaceful
The light white clouds, the mountains and the quiet fertile soil
All are pulsating in my blood.
The streams dance on the rocks, and the ancients sing heartfelt songs.

Tonight, I still have a traveler's dream
In which the eyes follow the fleeting ship
And I feel inexplicable happiness

115・

汴中元夕五首（其五）　　　　　李夢陽

細雨春燈夜色新，酒樓花市不勝春。
和風欲動千門月，醉殺東西南北人。

Five Poems About the Lantern Festival in Kaifeng (No. 5)　　Li Mengyang

Spring lanterns are brilliant in the
fine rain: a fresh night view; the wine

houses & markets of flowers are telling
the most telling spring. A gentle

breeze tugs at the moon from door
to door, which intoxicates wanderers

wandering from the north, from the
south, from the west, and from the east.

你的微笑　　　　　　　　　　　林明理

你的微笑，似橄欖林中的風
正好流入莫奈和他的花園上

而我不知道秘密是什麼
但我知道鳶尾花的香味
在最初的冬雪過後，便
從賽納河畔流到
我的書房

Your Smile   Lin Ming-Li

Your smile, like the wind from the olive grove
Blows into Monet's garden
Though I don't know the secret
I know the aroma of the irises
After the first winter snow, it drifts
From the banks of the Seine River
To my study

🌱 🌱 🌱

116 ·

重贈吳國賓   邊貢

漢江明月照歸人，萬里秋風一葉身。
休把客衣輕浣濯，此中猶有帝京塵。

Parting From a Close Friend   Bian Gong

The moon over the Han River
shines bright on my friend —

a returnee; autumn wind is blowing
through myriads of miles; wafting,

wafting is a leaf of your body.
Back home, please refrain from

washing your clothes, which are
stained with dust rolling in the capital.

請允許我分享純粹的喜悅 　　　　林明理

請允許我分享純粹的喜悅，
當暮色沉降
　　世界苦難無法舒解，
請允許我從風雪森林中
步向妳，像所有星辰，
像老橡樹靜靜守護更迭歲月。
沒錯，我將用魔法
　　把時間和空間凝結！
從現在出發——
　　且超過未來！

Please Allow Me to Share the Pure Joy
Lin Ming-Li

Please allow me to share the pure joy
When dusk is down
The suffering of the world cannot be relieved
Please allow me from the snowy forest
To walk toward you, like all the stars
Like the old oak tree quietly guarding the flight of years
Yes, I will use magic
To freeze time and space!
Now come on —
Go beyond the future!

117 ·

題美人　　　　　　　　　　　　邊貢

月宮秋冷桂團團，歲歲花開只自攀。
共在人間說天上，不知天上憶人間。

To a Beauty　　　　　　　　　　Bian Gong

The moon palace is cold in
autumn with masses of cassia

flowers, leisurely blossoming
from year to year. In the human

world, heaven is talked about
and admired, without knowing

that the moon cherishes a fond
memory of the human world.

倒影　　　　　　　　　　　　　林明理

霧靄淡煙著
河谷的邊緣，
你的影子沉落在夕陽
把相思飄浮在塔樓上。

回首，凝視那常春藤的院落。
每當小雨的時候

淚光與植物，混合成
深厚而縹緲的灰色⋯

The Inverted Image   Lin Ming-Li

The mist and pale smoke
The edge of the valley
Your shadow sinks in the setting sun
To float the lovesickness onto the tower

Looking back, gazing at the yard choked with ivy
Each time it rains
Tears and plants mix into
A deep and ethereal gray…

118 ·

送蕭若愚   邊貢

送君南下巴渝深，予亦迢迢湘水心。
前路不知何地別？千山萬壑暮猿吟。

Seeing My Friend Off   Bian Gong

Seeing my friend off, bounding for
the deep south, I also have a long

way to go, meandering with hills
and rills. The way ahead, where

will we part from each other?
Thousands of mountains and myriads

of ravines, at dusk, are resounding
with the sad cries of the monkeys.

在愉悅夏夜的深邃處　　　　　林明理

從未忘記。
風雨摧蝕的
　山海灣，
迎接耳語的浪花，
我們並肩跑往
　遼闊的星野。

背後的風
古老漁村的想像——
　恰如一個夢，
這路徑，錯落的腳印
　和笑聲。

而今
在記憶中逐漸抹去的，
　不是你逐浪的身影，
而是小小的思愁
　隨波成藍色……
忽遠，又靠近了。

林明理　油畫

In the Depth of a Pleasant Summer Night
Lin Ming-Li

Never forgettable
Is the weathered

Mountain bay
　　Greeting the whispering waves
　　We run side by side
Into the boundless starry field

　　The wind behind us
　　The imagination of an ancient fishing village —
Like a dream
　　The path, the footprints
And laughter

　　Now
　　What gradually fades away from memory
Is not your unrestrained form
　　But the lingering longing
Flowing with the blue waves……
　　Now far, and then near

❀ ❀ ❀

119 ·

題畫　　　　　　　　　　　　　　沈周

碧水丹山映杖藜，夕陽猶在小橋西。
微吟不道驚溪鳥，飛入亂雲深處啼。

Inscription on a Painting　　Shen Zhou

Holding a walking stick, I stroll
leisurely by green water babbling

in crimson mountains; the setting
sun is lingering and hanging to the

west of the small bridge. I ramble
while murmuring and crooning

― a bevy of birds are startled
into flight over the stream which,

chirping and twittering, fly into
the depth of clouds beyond clouds.

西子灣夕照 林明理

你的影像在
礁石浪潮中,
風甜甜地吹,
引我的思緒
留駐於心的記憶;
我記得
平灘上的每一足跡,
像今夜星辰般溫暖。
而我又告別了夕陽,
在大片天際線之下。

The Sunset at Sizihwan Lin Ming-Li

Your image is in the waves
Among the reefs
The wind blows sweetly
Tugging at my thoughts
The memory stays in my heart
I remember
Each footprint along the beach
Is warm like the stars of tonight
I again bid farewell to the setting sun
Under the vast skyline

120 ·

秋閨 　　　　　　　　　　　　　　　　　謝榛

目極江天遠，秋霜下白蘋。
可憐南去雁，不為倚樓人。

The Autumn Boudoir 　　　　　　Xie Zhen

The gaze is stretching —
far, and afar: autumn frost

descends over the white
duckweed. Lamentable:

the southbound wild geese
are not flying for those

who lean against the
balustrade of the tower.

我如何能夠… 　　　　　　　　　　　林明理

層層舞弄的浪花帶著寒意，
在潮汐間閃現記憶
激起漣漪——
在時光的蒼老中，
仍是幸福的。

噢，我如何能夠忘懷妳…
就像蒼蒼白濤，
不斷湧向彼岸——
只有明月馳過那片湛藍，
同欽慕的星光。

How Can I…   Lin Ming-Li

Layers of dancing waves are with a chill
Flashing memories among the tides
Ripples are stirred-up —
In the aging of time
Still happy

Oh, how can I forget you….
Like the boundless white waves
Continuously surging towards the other shore —
Only the bright moon glides through the azure blue
And the admired starlight

🌿 🌿 🌿

121．

春日雜詠   高珩

青山如黛遠村東，嫩綠長溪柳絮風。
鳥雀不知郊野好，穿花翻戀小庭中。

Inspired in Spring   Gao Heng

The green mountain, like a black
pigment, looms distantly to the

east of the village; tenderly green
lanky willows are dancing over

the long stream veiled in masses
of fluffy catkins. Sparrows and

birds, not knowing the attraction
of the suburbs and outskirts, are

fliting and flying among and
through flowers in the courtyard.

當黎明時分   林明理

星月消隱碧空,
悅耳的鳥鳴和平野的風
混和著。陣陣稻香
在空氣中浮動;
我走上熟悉的路,
不再害怕會錯失什麼,
除卻你情真的信息,
充盈在彼此的眼中。

At Dawn   Lin Ming-Li

The moon and stars disappear from the blue sky
The melodious birds' twitters mixed with
The field breeze. Spells of rice fragrance
Are floating in the air
I step onto the familiar road
No longer dread losing anything
Except for the true message
Which fills each other's eyes

122．

詠竹 朱元璋

雪壓枝頭低，雖低不著泥。
一朝紅日出，依舊與天齊。

Ode to the Bamboo Zhu Yuanzhang

The twigs are bent
low under the load

of snow, yet not so
low as to touch the

mud aground. When
the red sun comes out

to shine, it is still growing
upward — heavenward.

山野的蝴蝶 林明理

　你是否來自遙遠的國度？
和我一樣，自由放任，
　飄過遠古的陸地，神秘的山谷，
　從崎嶇的海岸奔向福爾摩沙。

　是誰驅動著你？
讓你無視洪水和降雪，
　誰是那寄語相知者？
讓你輕輕飛動
　掠過無數個春光。

不,你是宙斯最精緻的巧思,
如此難以接近,
　　無感於淚水與世間的悲涼,
　　那掠過的身影,卻使我心張望。

The Mountain Butterflies　　　Lin Ming-Li

　Are you from a remote country
Like me, carefree
　　Wafting over the ancient land and the mysterious valley
　　Running from the rugged coast to Formosa

　Who motivates you?
For you to ignore the flood and falling snow
　　Who is your bosom friend?
For you to fly gently
　　Through the splendor of countless springs?

　No, you are the most exquisite ingenuity of Zeus
So inaccessible
　　Unaffected by the tears and sadness of the world
　　Your silhouette flitting by tugs at my longing heart

🍀 🍀 🍀

123・

東風　　　　　　　　　　　　　　　　朱元璋

我愛東風從東來,花心與我一般開。
花成子結因花盛,春滿乾坤始鳳台。

The East Wind   Zhu Yuanzhang

I love the east wind
coming from the east,

which blows open the
flowers like my flower

of heart. After flowering
fruits are born; here at the

Phoenix Terrace, spring begins
to fill the heaven and earth.

夏荷   林明理

帶著一種堅強的溫柔
從西湖中凝望
這個風月無邊的
琉璃世界

是翠鳥兒？還是岸柳拂袖
遊魚也永不疲乏的
簇擁向我

那亭台之月，悄悄披上煙霧
來看流水
就是看不盡
一絲凜然的
荷影
夜的帷幕裏的光點

Summer Lotus   Lin Ming-Li

With firm gentleness
Gazing from the Lake West
At the boundless world
Of glass

Is it a kingfisher, or the bankside willows kissing water
The tireless fish
Are crowding toward me

The moon above the pavilion is stealthily misty
Come to look at the running water
Never tired of watching
The most charmingly graceful
Form of lotus
The bright stars twinkling in the curtain of night

124·

新雨水   朱元璋

片雲風駕雨飛來，頃刻憑看遍九垓。
檻外近聆新水響，遙穿一碧見天開。

Fresh Rain   Zhu Yuanzhang

A blossom after another blossom
of clouds, in the wind, is flying

here; in no time all the fields
become shadowy. Beyond the

balustrade, raindrops are freshly
dripping and dropping, when

the blue sky, faraway and far-
flung, is gradually opening itself.

雨影 　　　　　　　　　　　　　林明理

山角之轉彎。於
古渡口的小鎮上
你
被風刮得
偏離了方向
突然　閃爍的電光
清晰地照出半面的
白髮

在樹影輕輕飄下
於午后
聽蟬鳴
於
一次次
蛻變之中
直到河水越來越急
你方驚醒：
雨還是雨，停在船頭
而晦暗下來的世界
已然重新點亮

元詩明理達千載
古今抒情詩三百首
漢英對照

The Shadow of Rain   Lin Ming-Li

The corner of the mountain
In the town of ancient ferry
You
Are blown off the course
By the wind
The sudden flash of lightning
Clearly reveals the white hair
To one side

The shadow of the trees floating down gently
In the afternoon
Listen to the cicadas
In
Once and again
The metamorphosis
Until the river is more and more rapid
And you wake up:
The rain is still the rain, stopping at the bow
And the darkened world
Is re-lit

125・

金雞報曉   朱元璋

雞叫一聲撅一撅，雞叫兩聲撅兩撅。
三聲喚出扶桑日，掃盡殘星與曉月。

The Crow of the Rooster as Harbinger of Dawn Zhu Yuanzhang

The rooster crows
once aloud; the rooster

crows twice noisily;
the rooster crows thrice

resoundingly — and
all the remnant stars

are swept away, along
with the morning moon.

走在砂卡噹步道上 林明理

1.
走在砂卡噹步道上,
徐徐鋪展的歷史文字,
是盛開的野百合。

美麗的白䳍鴒,
還有迢迢遠方的
潺潺鳴響,
像是訴說著
無數勇士的故事。

2.
徜徉在中橫公路,
燕子母親們
在我頭頂的上空盤旋,
一隻大冠鷲的鳴叫,
是最詩意的回聲。

哦，所有的蟲鳥
都聽見我親切的問候，
知我喜歡太魯閣⁴⁹的黎明。

Walking Along the Shakadang Trail

Lin Ming-Li

1.
Walking along the Shakadang Trail
The slowly spreading historical words
Are wild lilies in full bloom

The beautiful white wagtails
And the dim and distant
Gurgling sound
Seems to be telling
The stories of countless warriors

2.
Wandering along the Zhongheng Highway
Swallows as mothers
Are hovering over my head
The cawing of a great crested vulture
Is the most poetical echo

Oh, all the bugs and birds
Have heard my cordial greetings
They know I like the dawn of Taroko.⁵⁰

---

⁴⁹ 太魯閣位於臺灣花蓮縣。
⁵⁰ Taroko is located in Hualien County of Taiwan.

126 ·

無題   朱元璋

天為帳幕地為氈,日月星辰伴我眠。
夜間不敢長伸腳,恐踏山河社稷穿。

Without a Title   Zhu Yuanzhang

The sky as the curtain and
the great earth as the carpet;

the sun and the moon and
the stars accompany me in

my sleep. Through the night
I dare not stretch my feet,

for fear that I trample and
tread on the hills and rills.

大貓熊[51]   林明理

在高山陡坡的密竹林中
    周圍是一片柔和
他攀爬,翻滾奔跑
酣睡的呆萌模樣
    彷彿夢見了奇異的珍寶

---

[51] 大貓熊 Giant Panda 主要棲息地是中國四川、陝西和甘肅的山區,是中國國寶。牠們已在地球上生存了至少 800 萬年,被譽為生物界的活化石。

元詩明理接千載
古今抒情詩三百首
漢英對照

大貓熊 Giant Panda
林明理 畫作

The Giant Panda[52] Lin Ming-Li

In the dense bamboo groves along steep slopes
The surrounding areas are soft and tender
He runs, rolls and climbs
Adorably and lovably sleeping
As if dreaming of a rare treasure

❀ ❀ ❀

127 ·

罵文士 朱元璋

嘰嘰喳喳幾隻鴉，滿嘴噴糞叫呱呱。
今日暫別尋開心，明早個個爛嘴丫。

To Curse the Literary Men Zhu Yuanzhang

Chittering and chattering,
a few crows, foul-beaked,

---

[52] The giant panda's main habitat is Sichuan, Shaanxi and Gansu mountain areas in China, and it is a national treasure. It has survived at least 8 million years on earth, known as the living fossil of the biological world.

are talking while revealing
the rough side of the tongue.

Today, please do not be
funny and make fun —

tomorrow, watch your
beak: it may go rotten.

一則警訊 　　　　　　　　　　　林明理

在世界地圖上
我看到未來
　繁星依舊
一座座冰山消融
陸地面積縮小了
當生物面臨飢餓
家園被毀時
哪裡有歸路可尋
哪裡才能避免不滅絕
　就這樣
隨著大地脈搏的跳動
　心跟著澎湃洶湧

A Warning Sign 　　　　　　Lin Ming-Li

On the world map
I see the future
The clusters of stars are still there
One after another iceberg are melting away
The land area is shrinking
When the creatures are facing hunger

When the homes are being destroyed
Where to find the road of return
How to avoid extinction
　　　Thus
With the heart beating of the earth
The heart is excitedly surging

128·

詠菊　　　　　　　　　　　　　　朱元璋

百花發時我不發，我若發時都嚇殺。
要與西風戰一場，遍身穿就黃金甲。

To Chrysanthemums　　Zhu Yuanzhang

A hundred flowers are
blossoming in spring, but I

refuse to do so; when I blossom
in autumn, all the other flowers

are overshadowed and overawed.
A battle, a fight with the west

wind — to do, or to die:
in golden armor I am robed.

東華大學校園印象　　　　　　　林明理

我漫步在偌大的校園
　　瞥見了藍天，三五野鴿
　　還有一片翠綠
在這一刻　寧靜的感覺裡
我偏愛草坪上的彩繪河流
　　景觀橋上　久久地佇立
我偏愛夢幻似的東湖
樹林群和多重魅力的建築
塵世的喧囂　遠遠離去
　　風舞山巒　陽光愜意

Impression of the Campus of Donghua University　　Lin Ming-Li

I stroll in the huge campus
　　Catching a glimpse of the blue sky and a few wild pigeons
　　　As well as a stretch of green
At this moment of tranquility
I love the painted river landscape on the lawn
　　On the landscape bridge　standing for a long time
I prefer the dreamlike East Lake
The clusters of forests and buildings of multiple-layered charming
The mortal clamor　far away
The wind blowing over the mountains　the sunshine is at ease

元詩明理垂千載
古今抒情詩三百首
漢英對照

129 ·

無題　　　　　　　　　　　　　　　　　朱元璋

諸臣未起朕先起，諸臣已睡朕未睡。
何以江南富足翁，日高三丈猶披被。

Without a Title　　　　　　　　　Zhu Yuanzhang

All the misters are asleep,
I wake and get up; all

the misters are asleep,
I stay awake to work.

The wealthy people in
the Southern Shore are

enviably in their bed when
the sun is high up in the sky.

洪患　　　　　　　　　　　　　　　　　林明理

沒有人能躲過
　　那突如其來的災禍
一排排汽車
　　如玩具般飄浮著
大量龍捲風和強降水
　　　　道路和住宅被淹沒
地球輻射平衡的變化與危害
讓人類生命，感到無所適從

Flooding
Lin Ming-Li

    Nobody can escape
The sudden disaster
    A row after a row of vehicles
Are floating like toy ducks
    A lot of tornadoes and heavy rainfalls
    To flood the roads and houses
    The change of the earth's atmosphere
    Has affected human life, rendering a sense of loss

130·

拜年
文徵明

不求見面惟通謁，名紙朝來滿敝廬。
我亦隨人投數紙，世情嫌簡不嫌虛。

Pay a New Year Call
Wen Zhengming

A New Year call is paid through greeting cards, instead of a face-

to-face meeting; in the morning, my humble house is filled with

a variety of cards. I follow their doing by sending greeting cards

whose mailing speed in favored, instead of scorning the formalities.

為義大利詩壇樹起了一面精神昂揚的旗幟
——寫給《PEACE》詩集
　　　　　　　　　　　　　　　　林明理

我知道這世界
有時很荒誕，有時很溫柔
但我從不感孤獨
因為在遠方，有你
遞來一曲曲吹奏的詩歌
它讓無邊無際的愛
貫穿於山川一切
從海的那邊到來[53]

Raising a High-Spirited Banner of the Italian Poetry Circle— For the Poetry Collection Entitled *PEACE*
　　　　　　　　　　　　Lin Ming-Li

I know the world
Is sometimes absurd, and sometimes tender and gentle
But I never feel lonely
Because in the distance, you are there
Travelling here one after another piece of music as poems
For the boundless love

---

[53] 承蒙義大利詩人、出版家 Giovanni Campisi 在去年底主編這本英義的雙語詩集《PEACE》，讓三位作者都得以唱出一曲曲感人心弦的歌。特別是詩人 Prof. Ernesto Kahan 飽經戰爭及病痛的磨難，仍毫不畏懼地寫出了引人動容的詩句:「We are the critical mass,／Nothing can stop us.」，揭示其生命的真諦，心靈高貴而又不凡。能與他們合著此書，不但給喜歡閱讀詩歌的讀者打開一個眺望世界的窗，也能感悟人生與愛情的優美境界。因而，我為此詩集萌生了感恩，也願它在義大利詩壇上放出光彩。

To be through the rivers and mountains
From beyond the sea[54]

🌿 🌿 🌿

131 ·

夜宿廬山　　　　　　　　　　　　楊慎

老夫今夜宿廬山，驚破天門夜未關。
誰把太空敲粉碎，滿天星斗落人間。

Lodging in Lushan Mountain　Yang Shen

I lodge, tonight, myself in
Lushan Mountain, where the

heavenly gate, startled and
frightened, remains unclosed.

Who tears the vault of heaven
into bits and pieces: a skyful

---

[54] Thanks to the Italian poet and publisher Giovanni Campisi, who edited this English-Italian bilingual poetry collection PEACE at the end of last year, the three authors were able to sing touching songs together. In particular, poet-professor Ernesto Kahan suffering through war and illness, but he is still fearless and has written a touching poem: "We are the critical mass, / Nothing can stop us", revealing the true meaning of his life. The soul is noble and extraordinary. Being able to collaborate to write this book with them not only opens a window to the world for readers who like reading poetry, but also allows them to understand the beautiful realm of life and love. Therefore, I feel grateful for this collection of poems and hope that it will shine in the Italian poetry world.

of stars are falling, through
the air, to the human world.

大安溪夜色 　　　　　　　　　　林明理

溪谷傳來樂音，
鳥獸無言。
多美的母親之河！
果樹芬芳，
無所畏懼外界的一切。

再遠的故鄉，
我都看得見。
多美的瀑布，
多美的梯田。
多美的織作——祖靈之眼[55]，
多美的紋面。

願我們部落與
另一端泰雅人，
都會永遠相伴相隨。
在山城，在溪畔，
啊，這歡愉的夜。

Da-an River At Night 　　　　　Lin Ming-Li

The valley is aloud with music
Birds and beasts are silent
How beautiful is the mother river!
The fruit trees, fragrant, are unafraid of anything

---

[55] 泰雅人的織作中，最著名的祖靈之眼（Dowriq Utux Rudan），是以兩個菱形所構成像似眼睛般的幾何圖形，是代表泰雅人祖先對族人的凝視。

In spite of the distance of my hometown
I can see it
So beautiful is the waterfall
So beautiful are the terraces
So beautiful is the fabric — the eyes of my ancestors[56]
So beautiful is its texture

May our tribe and
The Atayal over the other side
Always go hand in hand
In the mountain city, by the stream
Oh, what a joyful night

🌱 🌱 🌱

132 •

尋胡隱君　　　　　　　　　　　　　　高啟

渡水複渡水，看花還看花。
春風江上路，不覺到君家。

In Search of a Recluse　　　　　　Gao Qi

A river after another
river is crossed; clusters

upon clusters of flowers
are admired. The road

---

[56] In Atayal's fabric, the famous ancestral eye (Dowriq Utux Rudan) is a diamond-shaped geometry, representing the gaze of the ancestors of the Atayal upon their descendants.

279

along the great river is
blown in spring wind,

when I, unknowingly,
reach your home.

永懷文學大師──余光中[57]　　　林明理

您是永恆的詩人
時時夢繫故國和
　　福爾摩沙的美好
今夜，星子為你讚美吟咏
歌聲裡的芬芳
　　在風中悠揚
　　在紅紅的耶誕花上
　　　　發著光

Eternal Memory of Yu Guangzhong as a Master of Literature[58]　　Lin Ming-Li

You are an eternal poet
Always solicitous about your native country
　　And the beauty of Formosa
Tonight, the stars sing for you
The fragrance in the songs
　　Is melodious in the wind
　　On the red Christmas flowers
　　　　Is shining

---

[57] 詩人余光中教授逝世於 2017 年 12 月 14 日，享年 90 歲。
[58] Poet-professor Yu Guangzhong died on December 14, 2017 at the age of 90.

133．

田舍夜舂　　　　　　　　　　　　　　　高啟

新婦舂糧獨睡遲，夜寒茅屋雨來時。
燈前每囑兒休哭，明日行人要早炊。

Husking Rice in the Night　　　　　Gao Qi

Husking rice, a young woman stays
up late into the night which is cold,

coupled with the beginning rain over
the thatched hut. By the dim lamp

she coaxes, time and again, her baby
to refrain from crying, since her man

is to be an early riser-wayfarer, and
she herself will do the morning cooking.

原野之聲　　　　　　　　　　　　　　　林明理

在空中
或諸神的腳步中
時而愉悅
時而靜靜晃動

我從不期待奇蹟
也不感嘆歲月如流
能誠實面對自己

真正去努力
是唯一的信靠
恰如這原野之聲
使我安詳無憂

The Sound of the Wilderness Lin Ming-Li

In the air
Or in the footsteps of the deities
Sometimes joyful
Sometimes quietly vibrating

I never expect a miracle
Nor sigh over the lapse of years
To be honest with myself
Making real efforts
Is the only resort
Like the sound of the wilderness
Which makes me calm and peaceful

134 •

宮女圖 高啟

女奴扶醉踏蒼苔，明月西園侍宴回。
小犬隔花空吠影，夜深宮禁有誰來？

Painting of a Maid-in-Waiting Gao Qi

A maid-in-waiting supports the tipsy
imperial concubine in walking along

the flowery path overgrown with
green moss; in the bright moonlight

they are back from a banquet
in the west garden. A little dog

is barking through masses of
flowers toward the shadow —

in such a deep night, in the palace
forbidden, who is the intruder?

金山寺[59]的陽光溢滿樹梢 　　　　　　林明理

金山寺的陽光溢滿樹梢——
看，周遭深綠與蔚藍，
井水清澈好似晨露。
龍王宮前，
是怎樣的飛天圖案，
讓遠古的一切，
發出熾熱之光！

啊，讓我走進你，
在雷峰塔前，
白娘子等待的石階上。
那兒有普納眾生的
寺僧，還有夜浴的星光
那兒萬籟俱寂——
但，透射出沉靜的本然。

---

[59] 金山嘉佑禪寺〈簡稱金山寺〉，位於鶴壁市區西北三公里處的黑山南側，寺前山峰建有雷峰塔，相傳是《白蛇傳》中法海禪師鎮白蛇之塔。

The Sunshine of Jinshan Temple[60] Fills the Treetops

Lin Ming-Li

The sunshine of Jinshan Temple fills the treetops —
Look, deep green and blue all about
The well water is as limpid as morning dew
Before the dragon palace
What kind of sky-flying pattern
For everything in ancient times
To emit scorching light!

Ah, let me approach you
Before Leifeng Pagoda
On the stone steps where the White Lady is waiting
There are the monks accepting all
Humans, and the stars of the night bath
There is no sound —
But, revealing the calm nature

135 ·

龍州

林弼

峒丁峒婦皆高髻，白筼裁衫青布裙。
客至柴門共深揖，一時男女竟誰分？

---

[60] Jinshan Temple is located in Hebi city of Henan Province, three kilometers northwest of the southern side of the Black Mountain, and the peak of the temple is Leifeng Tower, which is believed, according to legend, to be the White Snake Tower in *The Legend of White Snake*.

Longzhou

Lin Bi

When in Longzhou, do as the people
of Longzhou do: they are all crowned

with buns, wearing white clothes
and blue sarongs and, upon the

arrival of a visitor at the wicket gate,
they would bow profoundly to show

respect and welcome — who can
discern a man from a woman?

悼土耳其強震[61]

林明理

金色古堡
　在霜冷的大地上
　　轟然傾倒，

風　為變色的山河
　消逝的萬物
　　瘖啞……

哀鬱的天空
　和神父們
　　保持靜默。

---

[61] 2023 年 2 月 6 日清晨，發生在土耳其南部接壤敘利亞邊境的七點八級強震，死傷人數逾五萬、建築物倒塌十分嚴重；因而以詩祈禱。

我遠遠地聽到
一個土耳其男人說：
「我女兒的小手
──還在瓦礫裡」

夜寂寂
　　死亡的腳步
　　無聲無息

主啊，請祢垂憐
　　受難者在角隅
　　　慄鳥在廢墟

地鳴震撼百里，
　　天使的歌聲
　　讓月亮裹足不前

Mourning the Great Earthquake in Turkey[62]

Lin Ming-Li

The golden castle
　Tumbles down
　　Upon the frosty earth,

The wind, changed hills and rills
　Myriads of things vanished
　　All dumb······

---

[62] In the early morning of February 6, 2023, a 7.8-magnitude earthquake happened in southern Turkey bordering the Syrian border, killing and injuring over 50,000 people and the buildings are seriously collapsed, hence the poem as prayer.

The mournful sky
　And the priests
　　Remain silent.

I hear a Turkish man
In the distance say:
　"My daughter's hand
　—Is still in the rubble."

The night is still
　The footsteps of death
　　Are silent

Lord, please have mercy
　On the victims in the corner
　　Of the chestnut bird in the ruins

The earth is shivering through a hundred miles,
　The songs of angels
　　For the moon to hesitate

🍀 🍀 🍀

136·

談詩五首（其一） 方孝孺

舉世皆宗李杜詩，不知李杜更宗誰？
能探風雅無窮意，始是乾坤絕妙詞。

Five Poems on Poetry Writing (No. 1)
Fang Xiaoru

Li Bai and Du Fu are
universally taken as the

models of poets, but who
is the twin-poets' model?

If a poet can dip into the
art of poetry itself, the best

poems between heaven
and earth can be produced.

老師,請不要忘記我的名[63]　　　　　林明理

分別三十年
我無法忘記你
那已經變得蒼老的身軀
不要難過,老師
請不要忘記校園和莿桐樹
不要忘記您對我們的期許
您教我曾經同聲唸過的詞語
都變成了詩歌
在今天相見的時刻
您依然是一棵樹
而我是萌生的葉子
加路蘭空中
還迴盪著我們的歡聲笑語
我說:老師
請不要忘記我的名

---

[63] 今天終於與莿桐國小的高慶堂老師見面了,原來老師也搬到台東同女兒同住;但高齡八十五的老師已有健忘症候群。我請老師到福井日本料理吃飯,然後一起去看海。老師靜坐輪椅上……在岸邊的亭下,我們愉快地拍了照。老師看到了永不停息的浪花、綠島的輪廓,諦聽著海濤聲,神情動容。

我的詩像大海的濤聲
當您記起時
我在樹葉上寫師
您的雨露之恩
讓我得到榮譽和幸福

———2016.01.05.

Dear Teacher, Please Don't Forget My Name[64]

Lin Ming-Li

Separation for thirty years
I cannot forget your
Body which has become aged
Don't be sad, dear teacher
Please don't forget the campus and the parasol tree
Don't forget your expectations for us
You taught me the words ever read together
Now have become poems
At the moment of meeting today
You are still a tree
And I am a budding leaf
The air of Jialulan
Is still echoing with our joyful laughter
I say: dear teacher
Please don't forget my name

---

[64] Today I finally met Mr. Gao Qingtang from Tong Primary School. My teacher has also moved to Taitung to live with his daughter. But the 85-year-old teacher has amnesia syndrome. I invited my teacher to Fukui Japanese restaurant for dinner, and then we went to admire the sea. The teacher sat in a wheelchair... We happily took pictures under the pavilion on the shore. The teacher saw the never-ending waves and the outline of the green island, listening to the sound of the sea waves, his expression moved.

My poem is like the sound of the sea
When you remember
I write on the leaves
Your rain-and-dew-like grace
For me to get honor and happiness

January 5, 2016.

137 ·

談詩五首（其二）　　　　　　　方孝孺

前宋文章配兩周，盛時詩律亦無儔。
今人未識崑崙派，卻笑黃河是濁流。

Five Poems on Poetry Writing (No. 2)

Fang Xiaoru

The poems of Song dynasty
are commendable; at its height,

the poems are peerless in rhyme
and art. Nowadays people

know not the power of the
poetry school of Kunlun,

and they laugh at the Yellow
River for its turbid water.

邵武[65]戀歌   林明理

當你的面龐在我的記憶裡逐漸清晰
這個冬日開始變得意味深長
就在這天然奇峽
聽風聲長嘯,觀丹崖茂林
有時豪邁
有時悵惘
我在錦溪傍眺望
遠方竹筏漂流
時而飄忽林間
每一山巒鬱鬱蔥蔥
每一碧水透明潔亮
我迷失在曲溪逐浪之間
在生機勃勃的天馬峰
遙思太極的奇妙通玄
風起了
你的漫步是蓮波的模樣
在另一個時空裡微笑

Shaowu[66] Love Song   Lin Ming-Li

As your face becomes clear in my memory
The winter begins to mean something to me
In this strange canyon
Hear the wind roaring, watching the dense forest over Red Cliff
Sometimes heroic
Sometimes sad

---

[65] 邵武市位於中國福建省西北部,武夷山南麓。
[66] Shaowu City is located in the northwest of Fujian Province, China, at the southern foot of Wuyi Mountain.

I look afar by Jinxi Creek
The bamboo raft drifting
Sometimes drifting in the forest
Each mountain is lush and green
Each blue river is clear and transparent
I am lost in the surging waves
In the vibrant Tianma Peak
Free imagination of the wonders of the Great Ultimate
The wind is arising
Your walk is the appearance of lotus waves
Smiling in another time and space

138．

清明有感 　　　　　　　　　楊士奇

西江南望渺天涯，歲歲清明不在家。
蕩日飄風無定著，亂人情思是楊花。

Inspired at the Tomb-sweeping Festival
Yang Shiqi

Southward looking from the West River, which is running to the

horizon; from year to year, I absent myself from home at the Tomb-

sweeping Festival. The sun is wafting and the wind is fleeting

without any destination; what
troubles the wanderer's mind

is the poplar filaments, which
are dancing, tumbling, lingering.

獻給敘利亞罹難的女童[67] 　　　　　林明理

再無人可以讓我哭泣
噢，我甜美的小女孩
如何讓妳重新唱歌
拂拭妳靈魂的憂傷
如何讓妳再度甦醒
默默地迎著親人走來

杏枝上掛滿了烏德琴
好似我流不住的淚
匯成空中的條條雨絲
讓我再貼近妳的小臉
比任何人都親
比任何人都把妳掛念

Dedicated to the Girls Killed in Syria[68] 　　Lin Ming-Li

Nobody can make me cry
Oh, my sweet little girl
How to get you to sing again

---

[67] 最近看到電視上有白盔志工男兒流下激動的淚，抱著救出的敘利亞小女孩罹難的身軀，很感傷，因而為詩。
[68] recently when I see on TV the white helmets in the war zone shedding hot tears while embracing the bodies of the girls killed in Syria, I feel sentimental, hence this poem.

To wipe away the sadness of your soul
How to make you awake again
Quietly to come while greeting your beloved ones

Apricot trees are covered with Oud
As if my running tears cannot stop
To form a line after another line of raindrops
Let me again get close to your little face
Closer than anyone else
I miss you more than anybody in the world

139·

劉伯川席上作 　　　　　　　楊士奇

飛雪初停酒未消，溪山深處踏瓊瑤。
不嫌寒氣侵入骨，貪看梅花過野橋。

Composed at the Banquet of Liu Bochuan
Yang Shiqi

The flying snow stops its flying
and the hangover is still massive;

in the depths of the mountain babbling
with streams, patches of snow are

found here and there. In spite of
the bone-penetrating cold, infatuation

with and admiration of plum flowers
bring me across the wild bridge.

給普希金 Aleksandr Pushkin   林明理

你漫步山之巔，領受明淨的風雪
在我臨近繆斯最美麗的邊緣
讓藍海、山溪、愛神、群星
為我們作證吧！
你深信光明必勝黑暗，而
我深信俄羅斯將永誌你的名！

To Aleksandr Pushkin   Lin Ming-Li

You walk atop the mountain, to receive the clear wind and snow
Upon approaching the most beautiful edge of my Muse
Let the blue sea, the mountain stream, love deity, and the maze of stars
Bear witness for us!
You are convinced that light will triumph over darkness, and
I am convinced that Russia will always honor you with your name!

揚州   曾棨

翠裙紅燭坐調笙，一曲嬌歌萬種情。
二十四橋春水綠，蘭橈隨處傍花行。

Yangzhou　　　　　　　　　　　Zeng Qi

Green skirts and red candle,
sitting and adjusting the reed

pipe wind instrument; a melodious
song is aloud with amorous

feelings. Under Twenty-Four
Bridge the spring water is

green, on which the oar is pulled
in and out of masses of flowers.

在高原之巔，心是如水的琴弦　　　林明理

我的生命如風
在高原之巔，心是如水的琴弦
一步近在腳下，一步一生遙遠
在菩薩之路[69]……我經過
一個又一個聖峰
無垠的草原與星野
我見過，佈滿風霜而平和的
也見過喜極而泣的臉
而你，青朴溪谷
像鏡般映射靈魂
你的歌裡，像雄鷹自由安祥
在人潮之間
有一種不同凡響的詮釋

---

[69] 每年朝聖者翻山越嶺、不辭辛苦地抵達大昭寺前，想見被供奉在裡面的釋迦牟尼佛，人們為他們掛上哈達，恭喜他們完成心願。對他們而言，抵達不是朝聖的終點，而是嶄新的開始。

Atop the Plateau, My Heart Is Like the Water-Like Strings
Lin Ming-Li

My life is like the wind
Atop the plateau, my heart is like the water-like string
One step is near me, another step is far away in life
Along the path of Bodhisattva[70].... I have passed
Through one after another holy peak
The boundless grassland and starry fields
I have seen faces covered with wind and frost
Yet peaceful, and faces crying with joy
And you, green valley alive with creeks
Like a mirror reflecting the soul
In your song, free and peaceful like an eagle
In the crowd of people
There is an extraordinary interpretation

🌳 🌳 🌳

141 ·

柯敬仲墨竹
李東陽

莫將畫竹論難易,剛道繁難簡更難。
君看蕭蕭只數葉,滿堂風雨不勝寒。

---

[70] each year, pilgrims cross the mountains and take the trouble to reach the Jokhang Temple to see the Buddha enshrined inside, and people hang Hada for them to congratulate them on fulfilling their wishes. For them, the arrival is not the end of a pilgrimage, but a new beginning.

An Ink Painting of Bamboo Li Dongyang

An ink painting of bamboo — easy?
Or difficult? One moment you

say free sketch painting is difficult
and the next moment, meticulous

painting is more challenging.
Look, only a few bamboo leaves

in the painting bring cold wind
& lashing rain which fill the room.

老橡樹 林明理

經過五百年,
您的額頭刻滿了風霜
以及所有走過艱難的圖式;
任何歌咏
也不能描繪唱讚──
您手臂上沾附著滿滿露珠,
在晨光下閃耀,使我多麼震動!
噢,上帝,
我飛翔的心……
獻上的不是浮誇,
而只是一首小小的詩歌,
猶如這夏夜的晚禱。

An Old Oak Lin Ming-Li

Through five hundred years
Your forehead is carved with wind & frost

And the traces of hardship
No song
Can adequately praise you —
Your arms are covered with dewdrops
Glistening in the morning light, so shocking to me!
Oh, God
My flying heart....
My offering is not extravagancy
But merely a little poem
Like the prayer in such a summer night

🍀 🍀 🍀

142 ·

梅花 　　　　　　　　　　　　　　寧王翠妃

鏽針刺破紙糊窗，引透寒梅一線香。
螻蟻也知春色好，倒拖花片上東牆。

Plum Blossoms 　　　　　Ning Wang Cuifei

An embroidery needle punctures
the window paster paper, to

induce a thready breath of
scented plum blossoms. The

ants, admiring the beauty of
spring, are dragging and drawing

the petals of plum blossoms
against the east wall of the house.

元詩明理建千載
古今抒情詩三百首
漢英對照

野桐

林明理

四月的清涼──終於讓這片野桐
唱起了歌。朝霧把山巒拂拭,
時間彷彿一瞬間過去了千年,而
我乘著歌聲的翅膀和你
重相聚首。
過去,我弄不清──你若有似無
神秘的微笑。
今天,我那麼近地將你端視
無視周圍的一切……
倘若你願意──我把你譜進
一支曲中。你會聽見我的傾訴
和我小鳥般的清鳴。

The Wild Parasol Trees

Lin Ming-Li

The cool of April — finally let this patch of wild parasol trees
Sing a song. The mist sweeps the mountains
A thousand years seem to pass in a moment, and
My wings of songs and you
Meet again.
In the past, I could not make it clear — your mysterious
Smile which seems to be and not to be
Today, I look at you so closely
Ignoring everything around me....
If you like — I'll put you in
A song. You'll hear my voice
And my chirping like a bird

143．

頌任公詩（其四）　　　　　　　歸有光

輕裝白袷日提兵，萬死寧能顧一生。
童子皆知任別駕，巋然海上作金城。

Ode to Ren Huan (No.4)　　Gui Youguang

In white robe and with light packs,
Ren Huan, a successful candidate

in the highest imperial examinations,
now is the leader of an army,

who chooses death before disgrace.
Even children know Ren Huan

as a general, who successfully
guards a fortified fortress.

朋友　　　　　　　　　　　　林明理

　　——就像北極星，
　無論我身處何地，
　　永遠知道彼此的距離。
　　無須鉅細靡遺地訴說，
　　沒有妒嫉，沒有猜疑，
　　在我心中閃耀著
　澄澈溫柔的記憶。

Friends   Lin Ming-Li

Like the lodestar
No matter where I am
We always know our distance
There is no need to tell in details
Without jealousy, without suspicion
My mind is brilliant
With memories which are clear and tender

144 ·

凱歌   沈明臣

銜枚夜度五千兵，密領軍符號令明。
狹巷短兵相接處，殺人如草不聞聲。

A Battle Song   Shen Mingchen

A wooden gag in the mouth
to ensure silence, five

thousand soldiers, receiving
orders, are marching by

night — a narrow lane,
fighting with cold steel,

killing each other like cutting
grass without any noise.

企鵝的悲歌[71] 　　　　　　林明理

在融解的冰層上
小小企鵝扭擺著身軀，茫然地徘徊
牠昂首呼喊，發出悲鳴，劃破寂靜的雪原

The Dirge of the Penguin[72] 　Lin Mingli

On the melting ice
A little penguin is twisting its body, wandering at a loss
It raises its head to utter a long, sad cry, piercing the silent snowfield

※ ※ ※

145・

蕭皋別業竹枝詞 　　　　　　沈明臣

青黃梅氣暖涼天，紅白花開正種田。
燕子巢邊泥帶水，鷓鴣聲裡雨如煙。

A Bamboo Branch Song 　Shen Mingchen

Green plums are mixed with yellow plums, red flowers with white flowers,

---

[71] 報載，南極出現生態慘劇，大型冰層將阿德利企鵝困在家園，150,000 隻企鵝因而踏上不歸路。

[72] According to news report, 150,000 Adelie penguins were trapped in their homes.

when it is now warm and then cold
— the best time to till the land

and sow the seeds. Swallows are
nesting with their muddy beaks;

wood pigeons are cooing through
the boundless sheet of misty rain.

寫給曹植之歌（組詩）　　　　　　　　林明理

一

飄在冬凝橋的柳絲青青
　雨，不發一點兒聲音
閃閃爍爍的記憶
隨著你清韻之步
　流蕩，徘徊

遙思三國
夢裡的王孫在呼喚些什麼
　而暮暮朝朝的
曹植
　就這樣靠近了

我知道，你愛寂寞
　也將堅決地
哺養這片希望的田野
你呼喚，像勁風的蘆葦
　歌吧，搖醒江淮之夜！

二
秋日陵墓前古樹蔥蔥。

而你，
吟詠如壯士。

睡去的七步村多純真！
我却不願遺忘那年
土崗上出現了洞穴的史實。

登上八斗嶺。仰瞻。
啊我始終相信，你是
詩人中的詩人，不凡的一生。

A Song for Cao Zhi (group poems)
Lin Ming-Li

(1)
Floating over the winter bridge the willows are green
    The rain refuses to produce any sound
The twinkling memory
With your steps of pure rhyme
    Drifting, wandering

Remote thinking of the Three Kingdoms
In the dream what are the aristocrats calling
    And from morning to evening
Cao Zhi as a famous poet
    Thus is so close

I know that you love loneliness
    And will resolutely
Feed this field of hope
You call, like a reedy song in the wind
    Sing, awake the night of southern rivers!

(2)
In front of the mausoleum the ancient trees are lush in autumn
And you
Are singing like a warrior

The Seven-Steps-Village is so pure and naïve!
I don't want to forget that year
When the cave appeared in the hill

Climbing atop the Batou Ridge. Look up.
Ah, I always believe, that you are
The poet of poets, an extraordinary life

🍀 🍀 🍀

146 •

送妻弟魏生還里　　　　　　　　王世貞

阿姊扶床泣，諸甥繞膝啼。
平安只兩字，莫惜過江題。

Sending My Wife's Brother Back Home
Wang Shizhen

Your sister is crying while
lying prostrate in the bed, and

your nephews are weeping
while clinging to your knees.

Take, please take care — when
you cross the river and reach

home, remember, to write back
a letter to report your safety.

寫給鞏義之歌──致鞏義市　　　林明理

在遠方溫婉的春雨
和夢寐在你的光亮之中
我將串起的驚嘆
變成輕輕滑進海峽的小槳
直奔開拓紀念杜甫的故鄉，
在那裡，有百家的碑林
與寬闊的詩香
那清澈、悅耳的森林之歌
重覆著歡快的音節
一遍遍：
松柏，眾鳥，流泉──
在那裡，美是最奪目的。
而你
永遠在前進的風雨中
迎向光明的世界
你比想像更美好
你比春花更繁茂！

A Song for Gongyi ─ Dedicated to the City of Gongyi
Lin Mingli

The gentle spring rain in the distance
And the dream in your light
I string the wonders
And turn them into a small oar gently sliding into the strait
Straight toward the hometown commemorating Du Fu
Where there are hundreds of stone monuments

And broad poetry aroma
The clear and sweet forest song
Repeats the cheerful syllable
Time and again:
Pines, birds, flowing springs —
There, beauty is the most dazzling
And you
Are always moving forward in the wind and rain
To meet the bright world
You are better than what is imagined
You are more brilliant than spring flowers!

147 ·

戚將軍贈寶劍歌二首（其二） 王世貞

曾向滄流剷怒鯨，酒闌分手贈書生。
芙蓉澀盡魚鱗老，總為人間事漸平。

Two Poems About a Treasured Sword (No. 2)
Wang Shizhen

The treasured sword has ever
cleaved the raging waves to kill

the monster whale, which is
given to a scholar as a gift after

drinking to be drunk. The sword,
with the name of "Lotus",

is tempered with time, with
history — and peace on earth.

丁方[73]教授和他的油畫   林明理

你從高原和山脈中走出來
　為了每一道風景敘事
　　盡了畫家的責任
更為大地歌頌
　從陝北到絲路
　從黃土高原到千溝萬壑
那些畫面
　全納入心靈裡
也加注了藝術的深刻印象

2009 年，作者和丁方教授於佛光山美術館畫展中在其油畫前合影
The author with professor Ding Fang before his oil painting at an art exhibition.

Professor Ding Fang[74] and His Oil Paintings
     Lin Ming-Li

You come out of the plateau and the mountains
　To narrate each landscape

---

[73] 丁方 (1956-)，陝西人，現任中國人民大學藝術學院院長、教授，其作品曾在高雄佛光山寺美術館與其他中國知名畫家聯合展出。畫中的景觀是高僧到西方取經跨過千山萬水的必經地帶，而山峰的壯闊，著實給人以精神上的啟悟，讓我印象深刻。

[74] Ding Fang (1956-), a native of Shaanxi Province, P. R. China, is currently the dean and professor of the College of Arts, Renmin University of China. His works have been exhibited in Kaohsiung Foguang Shan Temple Art Museum together with other well-known Chinese painters. The landscape in the painting is a necessary place for the monk to cross thousands of rivers and mountains to learn from the west, and the grandeur of the mountain really gives people spiritual enlightenment, so that I am deeply impressed.

And to perform the responsibility of a painter
To eulogize the great earth
From northern Shaanxi to the Silk Road
From the Loess Plateau to thousands of gullies
These pictures
Are all incorporated into the mind
Added to the deep impression of art

148．

老病始蘇 　　　　　　　　　　　李贄

名山大壑登臨遍，獨此垣中未入門。
病中始知身在系，幾回白日幾黃昏。

Recovery From a Chronic Disease
Li Zhi

All famous mountains climbed,
and all great waters viewed, I am

trapped, in an advanced age,
between the enclosing walls.

Down with a disease, I come
to know that I am imprisoned,

to see the light and dusk repeat
themselves from day to day.

短詩一束　　　　　　　　　林明理

1.
三隻黑冠猴
咕咕……唧唧……
向同伴發信號。

2.
雪夜馱著我。
在星辰見證中
我輕吻了明月。

3.
從金角灣末端……
伊斯坦堡和海的
倒影，誘夕陽走下來。

4.
白霧迷濛中，
兩隻默行的小雪豹。
一幅白底帶黑點的水墨畫。

　　　　　　　　　　　——2024.10.4

A Group of Short Poems　　　Lin Ming-Li

(1)
Three black-crested monkeys
Cooing……cawing……
To send signal to their partners

(2)
The snowy night carries me on its back
In the witness of the stars
I gently kiss the moon

(3)
From the end of Golden Horn Bay……
The reflection of Istanbul and
The sea, coaxing the sunset down

(4)
In the misty white fog
Two little snow leopards are walking silently
An ink painting with black spots on a white background

October 4, 2024

149·

閿都城渴雨時苦攤稅 湯顯祖

五風十雨亦為襃，薄夜焚香沾禦袍。
當知雨亦愁抽稅，笑語江南申漸高。

Taxation in Spite of a Drought Tang Xianzu

A gift from heaven: good weather
for the crops, but it is now a rare

phenomenon; the night approaching
and invading, the emperor burns

joss sticks to pray for blessings,
and his imperial robe is soaked

in the smoke. The rain, afraid of
the taxation, hesitates to drop and

fall — thus explained Shen Jiangao,
a southerner, to his master years ago.

蝴蝶谷的晨歌 　　　　　　　　　　林明理

自由的風,不停地吹——
回到鹿鳴溪流的清晨
當星子消隱,我發現群蝶翩翩
光影搖晃在一片濃稠的翠綠中。

這些安靜的夢幻或芳香——
在扶桑花的山野間,無比親切,
而我不經意地聽見　布農耆老在
尋找兒時的歡樂和樹低語。

黃鵲鴿輕舞著,白雲挨著來唱歌,
紅嘴黑鵯交頭接耳,在林梢
啁啾呢喃,重複著…
重複著…調皮清脆的音調。

自由的風,不停地吹——
回到月光映照著優美的祭儀歌謠,
當夏蟬唧唧,循環往復,我聽見
有野鳥在看不見的群峰鳴叫。

有山脊懸在雲端,紅藜懸在田野,
更遠處,還有一座老橋墩,
它靜靜地佇立,重複著…
重複著…思戀故鄉的音調。

The Morning Song of Butterfly Valley
Lin Ming-Li

The free wind keeps blowing —
Back to the morning with deer producing voices by the stream
When the stars disappear, I find the butterflies
Fluttering and swaying in a thick green

These quiet dreams or aroma —
Are endearing among the hills of Hibiscus flowers
Inadvertently I hear old farmers' joys
In search of childhood and the whispers of trees

Yellow wagtails are dancing gently, white clouds come to sing
Red-billed black bulbul whisper to each other, atop the forest
Chirping and repeating…
Repeating… a crisp and mischievous tone

The free wind keeps blowing —
Back to the moonlight reflecting the beautiful ritual song
When summer cicadas chirp, in repetition, I hear
Wild birds chirping on the unseen peaks

There are ridges hanging over the clouds, red goosefoot hanging in the field
In the far distance, an old pier
Standing still, repeating…
Repeating… the tone of homesickness

150・

七夕醉答君東 　　　　　　　　　　　湯顯祖

玉茗堂開春翠屏，新詞傳唱牡丹亭。
傷心拍遍無人會，自掐檀痕教小伶。

Drunk at Double Seventh Festival
Tang Xianzu

Encircled with spring green screen
after screen of trees, my new residence

is filled with tea aroma, and the
words of Peony Pavilion are widely

spread as songs. Sorrowful — I
lean against a balustrade after

another balustrade — all in vain:
nobody is privy to my mind, and

I take up hardwood clappers to teach
the young players the art of singing.

北國的白樺——致謝冕教授　　　　　　林明理

北國的白樺
矗立崖上，
群雁親近
向它丈量。

如星光照影
在疾風中，——
昂首而歌
讓夜驚嘆。

人們鍾愛它
面容安詳，
我卻欣賞它
誦讀的音響。

——收錄古遠清編著《謝冕評說三十年》，海天出版社，中國・深圳，2014年初版，頁279。

A White Birch in the Northern Land
— to Professor Xie Mian

Lin Ming-Li

A white birch in the northern land
Stands on the cliff
Bevies of wild geese flying nearby
To measure it

Like the stars shining through the shadow
In the high wind —
To sing with a head held high
To bring wonders to the night

People love it
With a serene face
But I admire it
For its reading sound

附錄
Appendix

文、圖:林明理
Article and photo by Lin Ming-Li

夜讀蔡輝振詩集《思無邪》(林明理)
Night Reading *Innocent Thinking*, a Poetry Collection by Tsai Huei-Ching (Lin Ming-Li)

　　蔡輝振是一位學者詩人,也是以詩為生命的苦吟者。他是香港珠海大學文學博士、雲林科技大學漢學所退休教授。雖然他在國際魯迅研究會、教學與研究上,多年來已有不少文章和專著論及,但其詩詞卻不多見。

　　值此歲暮夜深之際,有幸拜讀了輝振兄親自相贈的一本詩集,不僅讀到了描繪他在內蒙古大學客座期間,總結兩個月的蒙古遊記所題的精彩詩句,也從中欣賞到了穿插其中的景物與多情感性的一面。

　　這本《思無邪》詩集的最大特色是情感真摯和詩詞並茂,可以說達到了「詩中有畫」的情境;詩句時而雄渾、豪放,時而清麗、婉約,讓人不禁細細品味。請看〈蒙古風光〉這首古詩,寫的是詩人的感情融匯在蒙古景物的懷抱中了:

元詩明理揉千載
古今抒情詩三百首
漢英對照

大漠荒涼瀉百里，草原碧綠望無圍。
兒女馬背曲傳意，牛羊低吟喚犢依。
鷹翅扶搖志萬里，蒼狼咆月話悲啼。
海沙聯袂襯成趣，落日江河映漾暉。

再如這首（濡沫相依），寫的是詩人在年輕時，曾與一個北大女孩相戀，在他們經歷遊黃山的生死、離別，數十年後，在此詩中寫道：

同為異客訪名山，濡沫相依生死間。
今日分離何夕見，情歸何處惹愁僝。

這首詩歌頌了愛情，也描繪了詩人曾有的誓約，並為她的形象，寫下這首（朱顏）：

小臉柔美映燭光，絲髮半墜垂肩膀。
雙眉深鎖思哪樁？兩眸回盼令痴狂。
耳耳垂珠福成雙，厚鼻黃潤貴財長。
朱唇半翹招遐想，露齒白暈擁夢鄉。

雖然他是以口語的方式直接地表現出來，但仔細品嚼仍可發現，是他經過精心錘鍊，以達到其抒情隱逸其中的藝術風格。這是他今生最純真的愛情的寫照，尤其是詩中的女孩，超群的美麗，在她淡淡憂鬱的回眸中，就更富有詩意了。

再如輝振心中所懷念的黃山，讀來確實帶有一種具體可感的形象。詩人借助於禮讚黃山之美，是以其感情體驗為底韻，真切動人的筆墨來寫出這首（黃山日景）：

晨曦山戀飄渺間，午金流峰入雲端；
夕霞暉落映山澗，晚磷孤光灑滿天。

此外，作者在內蒙古大學文學客座所題的（我依然是我），寄托了不少一生的回憶，寫得很美，也有豪邁氣息：

318

我雖飛越不同的天空,
然天空依舊是天空;
我雖跨過不同的大地,
然大地依舊是大地;
天從不因為誰而改變,
地從不因誰而不載;
初衷依舊是,我依然是我。

此書最後一頁,〈悔恨〉詩裡的最後一段:

歲月悠悠,白雲蒼狗,往事哪堪回首;
遙想前塵,看盡天涯,多少悔恨交加。
懷念往昔,餘暉相依,濡沫生死相許;
今登高樓,望盡蒼穹,明月笑我傻懵。
任光陰荏苒!光陰荏苒!

這是蔡輝振柔情的顯現,其所思念與傳達的,乃是愛情本身神聖的光輝,縱然年輕時的愛戀已隨江水飄向遠方,但此詩仍顯示出詩人本身的孤獨、志向高遠與揮灑不羈的個性,盡融於詩詞的張力與剛柔並濟之間。

昨天午後兩點,輝振偕同其妻遠從臺中風塵僕僕前來拜訪,暢談三小時後,又開著他的吉普車揚長而去。今夜,繁星璀璨,我在書桌前閱讀蔡輝振曾經是發明家、企業家,後來因經商失敗,奮發圖強,終於成為一位學者的故事,也拜讀了他譜出生命的旋律的詩詞。正如他的這首〈不可強求〉,詩的寓意是很明顯的:

生死有命,富貴在天;
凡事盡心,得失隨緣。

看來,愛情不僅給了他創作靈感,也引向了他對人生的思考與對生命的追求。以上這些記述蔡輝振旅遊、所見所思和愛情的詩詞，不論哪一種，律詩、絕句或古詩、現代詩，都形象生動地記錄了他一生的光輝及經歷。因而，此書也標誌著他一生生活的真實寫照，也是他晚年對詩詞創作及其較深的思想內涵的一種昇華，更具禪道韻味了。

2022.12.19 寫於臺東

——《金門日報》Kinmen Daily News，副刊，2022.12.30。

蔡輝振著《思無邪》，2020 年初版，臺中市，天空數位圖書版。

    Tsai Huei-Ching is a scholar-poet and a singer who takes poetry as his life. He is a Doctor of Literature from the University of Zhuhai in Hong Kong and a retired professor at the Institute of Chinese Studies of Yunlin University of Science and Technology. Although he has written, through so many years, many articles and monographs concerning the International Lu Xun Research Society as well as teaching and research, his poetry is a rare thing.

    On the occasion of the late evening of the New Year, I had the honor to read a book of poetry given by Mr. Tsai personally. I not only read the wonderful verses describing his travel notes in Mongolia for two months during his visiting period in Inner Mongolia University, but also enjoyed the scenes interspersed with them as well as his sentimentality.

The greatest feature of this poetry collection entitled *Innocent Thinking* is the combination of sincere emotion and poetry, which can be said to achieve the level of "painting in poetry". The poems are sometimes bold and vigorous, sometimes beautiful and graceful, entailing people to taste and savor. Please take a look at this ancient poem entitled *Mongolian Scenery*, which describes the poet's feelings being integrated in the embrace of Mongolian scenery:

> The desert is desolate and boundless,
> and the grassland is endlessly green.
> Children on horseback bend to convey,
> Cattle and sheep nursing their children.
> The wings of the eagle spread far and wide;
> The wolf is solitarily howling to the moon.
> The sea and sand are lined together for fun;
> The sunset over the river is on the rippling.

Another example is this poem entitled *Mutual Help and Relief*, which describes when the poet was young, he had fallen in love with a girl from Peking University. After they experienced the death and separation of in Mount Huang, he wrote, decades later, in the poem:

> As strangers we visit the famous mountain;
> Mutual help and relief between life and death.
> Today, separation; tomorrow, when to meet?
> The feeling, whom to tell? Whom to lean to?

The poem eulogizes love and describes the vows the poet once made, and for her image, a poem entitled *The Bloom of Youth*:

> A tender face against the candlelight,
> Fair long hair to reach her shoulders.
> Brows knitting, what is on her mind?
> Her backward glances, an infatuated heart.

Ears drooping with pearls and blessings;
A thick nose foretells a good luck and fortune.
Her red lips half cursed up, charmingly sexy;
Her white teeth revealed, like a fond dream.

Although he directly expresses in a colloquial way, a careful examination can find that he has been carefully honed to achieve his lyrical seclusion in the artistic style. This is the portrayal of his purest love in this life, especially the girl in the poem, the stunning beauty, in her light melancholy eyes, it is more poetic.

Again, Mount Huang which Tsai misses in his heart is indeed read with a specific image that can be felt. With the help of praising the beauty of Mount Huang, the poet wrote this poem *The Day View of Mount Huang* with a vivid and moving brush and ink based on the emotional experience:

Morning light is ethereal through mountain mist;
The afternoon gold flows over the peak into clouds.
The rosy clouds of the setting sun reflected in mountains,
The evening phosphorus and solitary light fill the sky

In addition, in *I Am Still Me*, written by the author at the Inner Mongolia University, a host of his memories are recorded — written beautifully, and not without a heroic breath:

Though I fly through different skies,
the sky is still the sky;
though I cross different lands,
the earth is still the earth;
the days never change for anybody,
the earth never refuses to nurse anybody;
the intention still remains: I am still me.

The last page of the book, the last paragraph of the poem entitled *Regret*:

The years are long, white clouds and dogs, the past cannot be looked back;
Thinking of the former existence, see to the horizon, how many regrets.
Cherishing the past, lingering afterglow, mutual help and relief in life and death;
Climbing the tower, gazing at the sky, the moon laughs at my infatuation.
Time — flies! Time, times!

This is the manifestation of Tsai Huei-Ching's tender feelings, and what he misses and conveys is the sacred glory of love itself. Even though the love in his youth has drifted away with the river, this poem still shows the poet's own loneliness, ambition and unrestrained personality, which is fully integrated in the tension and hardness of the poem.

At two o'clock yesterday afternoon, Tsai and his wife came from Taichung to visit me, and after talking for three hours, they drove off again in his jeep. Tonight, the stars are shining, I read in front of the desk the story of Tsai Huei-Ching who used to be an inventor and entrepreneur, and later owing to business failure, he worked hard, eventually to become a scholar. I also read his poems running with the melody of his life. As in his poem *Not to Be Forced*, the moral of the poem is obvious:

Life and death is fated; wealth and poverty is by heaven.
All things without sparing efforts, gain and loss, let it be.

It seems that love not only gave him creative inspiration, but also led to his thinking about life and the pursuit of life. The above poems describing Tsai Huei-Ching's travel, vision and love, no matter what kind of poems, quatrains or ancient poems, modern poems, all vividly record the glory and experience of his life. Therefore, this book also marks the true portrayal of his life, and is also a sublimation of his poetry creation and its deeper ideological connotation in his later years, with more charm of Zen.

December 19, 2022, written in Taitung
The supplement of *Kinmen Daily News* dated December 30, 2022

國家圖書館出版品預行編目資料

元詩明理接千載——古今抒情詩三百首（漢英對照）/
林明理 著、張智中 譯 －初版－
臺中市：天空數位圖書 2024.11
面：14.8*21 公分
ISBN：978-626-7576-02-1（平裝）
831　　　　　　　　　　　　　　　　113016919

書　　名：元詩明理接千載——古今抒情詩三百首（漢英對照）
發 行 人：蔡輝振
出 版 者：天空數位圖書有限公司
作　　者：林明理
譯　　者：張智中
美工設計：設計組
版面編輯：採編組
出版日期：2024 年 11 月（初版）
銀行名稱：合作金庫銀行南台中分行
銀行帳戶：天空數位圖書有限公司
銀行帳號：006—1070717811498
郵政帳戶：天空數位圖書有限公司
劃撥帳號：22670142
定　　價：新台幣 500 元整
電子書發明專利第 I 306564 號
※如有缺頁、破損等請寄回更換　　　　　版權所有請勿仿製

服務項目：個人著作、學位論文、學報期刊等出版印刷及DVD製作
影片拍攝、網站建置與代管、系統資料庫設計、個人企業形象包裝與行銷
影音教學與技能檢定系統建置、多媒體設計、電子書製作及客製化等
TEL　：(04)22623893　　　　　　MOB：0900602919
FAX　：(04)22623863
E-mail：familysky@familysky.com.tw
Https ://www.familysky.com.tw/
地　　址：台中市南區忠明南路 787 號 30 樓國王大樓
No.787-30, Zhongming S. Rd., South District, Taichung City 402, Taiwan (R.O.C).